I've travelled the world twice over,
Met the famous: saints and sinners,
Poets and artists, kings and queens,
Old stars and hopeful beginners,
I've been where no-one's been before,
Learned secrets from writers and cooks
All with one library ticket
To the wonderful world of books.

© Janice James.

The wisdom of the ages
Is there for you and me,
The wisdom of the ages,
In your local library.

There's large print books
And talking books,
For those who cannot see,
The wisdom of the ages,
It's fantastic, and it's free.

Written by Sam Wood, aged 92

EMILY

Emily Brontë was the most enigmatic, the most individual and the most talented of all the gifted Brontë family. This novel tells the story of her life, set against the background of Haworth, her home which she loved, the gaunt moors which surrounded it, and the activities of herself, her brother and her sisters, from her birth to her death. But it is also the story of a mind developing and growing; of her probing into literature and the world of the metaphysical; of how she came to write her poetry, and especially of how she produced her great masterpiece WUTHERING HEIGHTS.

DILYS GATER

EMILY

Complete and Unabridged

ULVERSCROFT
Leicester

First published in Great Britain

First Large Print Edition
published 1998

British Library CIP Data

Gater, Dilys
Emily.—Large print ed.—
Ulverscroft large print series: general fiction
1. Large type books
I. Title
823.9′14 [F]

ISBN 0–7089–3976–7

Published by
F. A. Thorpe (Publishing) Ltd.
Anstey, Leicestershire
Set by Words & Graphics Ltd.
Anstey, Leicestershire
Printed and bound in Great Britain by
T. J. International Ltd., Padstow, Cornwall

This book is printed on acid-free paper

In loving memory of Janice.

Author's Note

I owe a great debt to the many books I have read on the subject of Emily and the Brontë family, particularly:

Emily Brontë by Winifred Gerin
The Brontës by Brian Wilks
Unquiet Soul by Margot Peters
The Brontë Story by Margaret Lane
The Infernal World of Branwell Brontë
    by Daphne du Maurier
The Brontës by Phyllis Bentley

And of course to the works of Emily and the Brontës themselves.

'Towards twelve o'clock, the pain grew worse, but I refused to go to bed or lie down. I have always believed that the will is stronger than the body, and there was so much still that I wanted to think about. It was difficult to bear the suffering on the faces of my sisters — they, I knew, suffered far more than I in watching my struggles for breath, but then they had never understood me, deeply though they loved me and I them.

'I found I was looking at them as though they were strangers. Charlotte, always the strong, the leader, the promoter in our ventures — and yet so weak in many ways. Wanting to manage me even now, when I was aware that my last hour was drawing near. Dear Charlotte! She thought earthly things would soothe, would comfort. That morning she had been out early, and had searched the moors for a sprig of heather to gladden my eyes when I woke. She knew how I had always loved the moors — but did she not understand that death the last, the greatest mystery of all, would unite me with them for ever? No need of a sprig of

1

heather when soon I would have unity with the mystic and the Absolute essence of nature that had dominated my life for so long.

'Yet though she thought I had not recognized the heather, the gesture remained, typical of Charlotte's physical warmheartedness. I recalled the many times her overflowing heart had led her into difficulty, and the love affair which had agonized her for two long years. Physical love. My heart bled for her. Poor Charlotte, so little equipped to face life upon this earth, her mind so limited by a desire for physical passion. Could I not, even at this late hour, give her some indication of the littleness of physical passion when confronted by the mighty sense of fulfilment with the passion of the soul? Yet how inadequate are these things we call words.

'I had tried, in my work, to give some indication of my feelings. Yet all — all had been discredited, derided, laughed at, caused consternation and horror, but this was my reality. Wuthering Heights was my testament, as near as I could get it in comparison with earthly terms, to the nakedness of spirit which underlies our earthly life as the rocks do the soft springing of the turf and heather on my dear moors. And I had found no kindred soul to share the knowledge with me, no

2

one who understood. Well, so be it. I would die, as I had lived, alone, strong in my inner convictions, unafraid of death except insofar as it grieved my sisters to watch my passing.

'They had recently lost Branwell, the brother who had come, perhaps, nearest to understanding me in his discovery that the world counts for nothing besides the immensity of Eternity and the Infinite. But the knowledge had frightened Branwell — he had been unable to face it — he had sought to hide from it in drink and drugs. His death had been pitiful. Mine, I vowed, would not be. I would go fearlessly, and carry out to the last the lines I had written:

''No coward soul is mine.'

'Yes, I would die bravely. I would accept death, embrace it. My first and only lover, come for me to show me the delights beyond the veil.

'Anne was not far from crying, but though gentle, her spirit burned like a candle flame, small, yet steadfast. There were depths to Anne's nature that Charlotte had never comprehended. How little we know of each other, separate as we are in our different bodies. We four — Charlotte, Branwell, Anne and I — had been close as brother and sisters have never been, almost as one person. And yet, we were not one, we were four, each an individual, each so very very different from his fellows.

'I felt the struggle for breath grow almost too much for me. I could not bear their sorrowing eyes any longer. Soon it would be time. Soon I would know all — understand all — be at one with the heavens and the stars and moons and planets that whirled about our little earth.

'I felt it in me that whatever happened now would come too late, so for their sakes, I gasped out to Charlotte:

''If you will send for a doctor, I will see him now.'

'And I lay down on the familiar old sofa — no use regretting that I had done so little with my life, that my passing would go unremembered except by a few dear sorrowing ones — to die.

'If only I could have done more — The past swam before me in a haze, but now, it was too late.'

1

Elizabeth Firth — or Beth, as her father called her — straightened up, smoothing the folds of her old blue muslin, which the baby, Branwell, had grasped in too tight a fist during their game.

'Look at that,' she said to Annie, the housekeeper, who had just come in with the tea, and indicated a large tear where the skirt had come away from the high-waisted bodice. She laughed. 'Good thing I put on an old gown.'

'He's a real boy, and no mistake,' pronounced Annie, setting down the tray, 'but Nelly'll soon mend it, Miss Beth. You sit down and have your tea quietly now, and I'll take the children into the kitchen for some milk and cake. You need a rest. You've been romping with them all afternoon.'

Beth loved the children, but she had to admit it was a little tiring looking after them, and thankfully, she sat down while Annie shooed the little girls, Maria, Elizabeth and Charlotte from the room, and picked up the baby, Branwell, who immediately began to howl. Beth smiled and shook her head.

He'd been laughing only a moment ago, thoroughly enjoying their game.

As his howls faded away in the direction of the kitchen, she became pensive. Poor Mrs Brontë would have another baby even younger to take care of now.

'Children are a blessing of marriage,' her best friend, Caroline Fairweather had said to her often, her eyes soft with a maternal light, for Caro adored children, and wanted at least ten — when she married. Surely, thought Beth, it must be rather a heavy burden, if your constitution was weak and delicate as dear Mrs Brontë's was, to have to produce a baby every year. It was really no wonder that Mrs Brontë looked so ill and pale. She had presented her husband with five infants in five years, including the latest, another little girl who had been born this very day.

'Oh!' exclaimed Beth, as a thought struck her, and she rose and hurried across to where she kept her diary, in the escritoire in the corner that was her own special property. She must enter the news of this latest happening without delay.

Leaving her tea cooling, she picked up a pen and turned to the right page. The year was 1818, and she wrote:

July 30th.
Emily Jane Brontë born.

Emily Jane. It was a pretty name, and a pretty baby, too, according to the servant who had rushed across only an hour ago to tell them that it was all over at the house in Market Street where the Brontë family lived, and that both the new baby and her mother were well.

Beth wondered whether Mr Brontë was pleased with his daughter. He already had a son to follow in his footsteps, and as Emily Jane was the fifth child, the birth of a baby was nothing new to him. Thinking of the year-old Branwell reminded Beth again of her torn dress, and she went pensively back to the tea-tray. Even though he was only a year old, Branwell was so strong and — well, she had to admit it — virile for a baby. He took after his father, who no doubt had been equally lusty when he was an infant. Now, he was a tall, handsome, charming man of forty or so, and Beth could imagine how Mrs Brontë had been swept off her feet by him, for although nobody knew about it except Caro, who knew everything, Beth herself treasured a secret passion for the good-looking clergyman.

'I don't think he's really as handsome as

all that,' Caro had pronounced judicially, when they were exchanging secrets, and Beth rushed at once to his defence.

'Well, of course, he's quite old now, but imagine what he was like when he was younger. I expect he was absolutely *devasting*.'

'You do see more of him than I do,' agreed Caro, turning up her pert nose as she studied herself in the hand-glass, looking for non-existent wrinkles on her young face.

Yes, indeed, thought Beth. She had offered to look after the little ones while the new baby was being born because she was genuinely fond of them — Maria, the eldest, like a little mother to the rest; Elizabeth, the shy one, who would nevertheless always put a hand confidingly into Beth's; plain little Charlotte, and the lusty young Branwell. In a way she felt a little sorry for them. Her father was the patron of the Bell Chapel here in Thornton, of which Mr Brontë was curate in charge, so naturally the families had quite a lot to do with each other socially, but the constantly recurring indisposition of Mrs Brontë meant that the family as a whole could not go out very often, so either the children or Mr Brontë came alone on most of their social calls. Beth's heart always fluttered whenever she saw that tall figure.

'I know what you mean, mine always does that when I see Mr Aynsley,' confided Caro, who also suffered from an unrequited passion for a much older and highly unsuitable gentleman. What each would have done if the gentleman in question had suddenly declared their love, Beth and Caro never worried about. They wanted an ideal to dream of at a distance, and for Beth, Mr Brontë fitted the bill admirably, especially as his own history, and that of his wife were romantic in the extreme. She was lively and curious, and she had made it her business to find out as much as she could about Mr and Mrs Brontë — or Patrick and Maria, as she called them in her own mind.

'Do you know, he was born in Ireland, in a place called Drumballyroney, and his family was terribly poor,' she told Caro impressively.

'Drumballyroney? I've never heard of it,' said Caro. Beth had to admit that she hadn't, either.

'Well, at any rate, his family was terribly poor, as I said, but do you know what he did? He educated himself and worked terribly hard and actually became a *teacher*. And then, he even went to Cambridge, and was there with Lord Palmerston. They thought there was going to be an invasion from France at the time, and he and Lord Palmerston formed a volunteer force at the college, and drilled together. I should love to have known him then,' said Beth, her face alight with pride.

'I don't think I should care for someone who was born into the lower classes. At least Mr Aynsley is a gentleman,' commented Caro, and Beth flushed with indignation.

'Well, so is Mr Brontë, now. I think it makes him all the more romantic — to think that he worked his way up in life like that. He had a terrible struggle to survive at Cambridge, as far as money went, I expect. I admire him all the more for it,' she said hotly.

'Oh, well, don't let's argue. What happened after that?' asked Caro, now genuinely interested, and Beth carried on with her tale.

'He graduated in 1806, and was ordained as a deacon, and in 1807, he was ordained as a priest, then he went to several different curacies. He must have been marvellously handsome then. I wonder if he broke any hearts,' she mused, 'I expect so. He really is charming, Caro, even now.'

'Yes, but I can't imagine any Mamas and Papas thinking he would be a very good match for their daughter, all the same,' said

10

Caro, thoughtfully. 'After all, he must have been awfully poor, and they wouldn't have cared however madly handsome he was.'

'Perhaps he has some secret love affair of bitter-sweet memory stored away from those long ago days. I'm sure he must have,' said Beth, dreamily.

'Well, he married Mrs Brontë, so it can't have been all that bitter-sweet, to remain with him for ever and keep him true to his one and only love,' Caro pointed out realistically. 'But of course — perhaps he wanted children.'

'I don't think he exactly *wanted* them, not then, anyway,' said Beth. 'I expect he was ambitious. He went to Wetherfield in Essex, and Wellington in Shropshire, and then Dewsbury up here in Yorkshire. And, oh, Caro, he was so brave! While he was a curate at Dewsbury, do you know what he did? All sorts of things. One time, a drunken man was trying to stop a children's Sunday School procession from passing, and Patrick — I mean Mr Brontë, just threw him into a ditch!'

'Did he really?' said Caro, fascinated.

'Yes, and then, when the procession was on the way back from church, the drunken man had got a group of his friends together, and they all barred the way.'

'Whatever happened? I should have died of fright,' said Caro.

'Patrick tackled them all, single-handed, and scattered the lot!' exclaimed Beth triumphantly. 'How brave he must have been, as well as handsome. Then, later on, things got worse. After Dewsbury, he became the Vicar of the Church of St Peter's at Hartshead — you know, Hartshead-cum-Clifton — and he was there when all those riots took place.'

'What riots?' asked Caro. 'Goodness, Beth, you make it sound quite like a story in a book.'

'Well, they were called the Luddite riots, I think,' Beth explained. 'All sorts of things were happening just then, and the workers in the mills and factories were very discontented. New machinery was being brought in, you see, which could do the work of many of the men at a time, and they were afraid for their employment. Then corn cost an awful lot to buy, and they weren't very pleased about the war with Napoleon — but it was the new machinery — they called them 'frames' — that really upset them, so they started to form groups and attack the 'frames' as they were being brought in. They even attacked the mill-owners as well. It must have been like a civil war, because, when things got

12

really bad, a detachment of cavalry was actually called for and sent to the district. Oh, Patrick's told me many tales of how some of the brave mill-owners — and they weren't all bad — held out under siege with loyal workmen against the Luddites, until the soldiers could come to their assistance.'

'Goodness gracious,' said Caro, staring. 'I'd never realized your Mr Brontë had led such an interesting life.'

'When he tells you about it, you can almost feel as though you were there,' said Beth, eagerly. 'You can feel how desperate the workers must have been, and how the military were determined to stamp out the riots at all costs, and the danger to the mill-owners, whose property was being destroyed — why, one of them was actually murdered — the mill-owners, I mean, and that led to a real hunting down of the rebels. Fourteen men were hanged at York, and others were sent to the prison hulks or for transportation. Patrick was in the middle of all of it, going about his duties. He bought a pair of pistols then, and he's still got them. He fires them every so often, just to make sure they're in working order. He told me.'

'My goodness,' said Caro. Then she pouted, 'Well, I suppose it's all very exciting, Beth, but I must say, I prefer *my* tales to have a bit of romance in them. Why, Mr Aynsley almost persuaded a young lady to elope with him. I think that's far more interesting.'

But Beth was not to be sidetracked.

'Don't you think it's romantic that Patrick is actually a published author?' she demanded, and showed Caro copies of Mr Brontë's books that he had presented to her himself, but Caro was not impressed.

'*Cottage Poems*,' she read. '*The Rural Minstrel*. Oh, they don't look at all thrilling. I like tales about mad monks and wild, exciting lovers, not poems like these.'

'But don't you see, they're not intended to be read by people like you,' explained Beth, the light of idealism in her eyes. 'Patrick wrote them for the poorer people, who haven't had much education. He feels that there's a great need for reading material for the under-privileged classes. I suppose he's thinking of his own background. And I think his concern for the poorer people's welfare shows that he's good and compassionate, as well as brave and handsome. I wish I could write books.'

Caro looked shocked. 'Ladies don't do things like that,' she exclaimed.

'I can't see why not,' said Beth. Then she sighed, 'except that I would never be able to think of anything to write about.'

14

'I always like romances,' sighed Caro, toying with her curls. 'Oh, I do hope a romance happens to me some day.'

'Patrick and Maria had a great romance — or at least, I'm almost certain they did,' said Beth.

'Did he tell you?' asked Caro, eagerly, and Beth shook her head.

'Oh, no, of course not, I've sort of pieced things together. Maria must have been really beautiful when he married her, so dainty and fragile. She always reminds me of a piece of delicate china. It's a pity that being ill all the time has spoiled her looks — although I expect she always looks beautiful to him,' she added sentimentally.

'I wouldn't exactly call her beautiful,' considered Caro. 'Pretty, yes, but what happened?'

'Well, it was when Patrick was at Hartshead,' began Beth, settling herself more comfortably. 'I've worked out that he must have been thirty-five when he met her. Her name was Maria Branwell, and she comes from Penzance, in Cornwall.'

'How did he come to meet her, then?' asked Caro.

'She was staying with her uncle, the Reverend John Fennell, and his wife, and they met through the Fennells' daughter, Jane.

She'd just become engaged to a great friend of Patrick's, the Reverend William Morgan, and Patrick and Maria met in the August of 1812, and had a whirlwind courtship.'

'How do you know it was whirlwind?' demanded Caro, now completely absorbed.

'Well, it must have been,' argued Beth. 'They were married in the December. They had a double wedding with Jane and William. They must have been madly in love. I mean, think of the difference in their backgrounds. Maria was a lady born, and she was used to a very genteel sort of life in Cornwall — and she gave it all up to live in a harsh sort of countryside, on not much money, and of course — well, being married, she's had all these children, and that can't have been much fun for her, when she was used to a social round.'

'I'd do it all if I met somebody I was passionately in love with,' declared Caro. 'Even if he was a — a — well, I don't know. And I'd love my children. I don't think you can be very maternal, Beth.'

'I suppose they're all right once they're *there*,' said Beth, consideringly. 'It's the having of them that seems so wearisome. Poor Mrs Brontë's never really well. I wonder whether she's happy?'

'I expect so. She must have known what

she was doing when she gave everything up for love,' said Caro, 'and after all, she's married to your darling Patrick. Wouldn't you give everything up for him?'

'I've never thought about it,' admitted Beth. 'Oh, Caro, what a scandalous conversation. Young ladies shouldn't even think about things like that.'

'Why not? That's what life's all about. Anyway, nobody will ever know what we've been saying,' said Caro, comfortably.

Beth thought about that conversation now, as she sipped her tea. Perhaps, she thought, Maria had always longed for children, as women were supposed to do. She tried to imagine herself married, with a new baby every year, living on a modest income instead of in the luxury to which she was accustomed, and with a husband who shut himself in the parlour to write books all the time — for since settling at Thornton, Patrick, who was still writing, had published two more works, *The Cottage in the Woods* and a prose tale, *The Maid of Killarney,* or, *Albion and Flora.* Would everything be worth it for love? Beth found herself mazed. In spite of her conversations with Caro, her imagination, as with most unmarried young ladies, carried her to the altar, but no further.

She debated the matter, and finally decided that even if the handsome Patrick was free, and proposed to her, she would definitely think twice about giving up the luxury and gentility of her home in order to marry him.

She heaved a sigh. So much for romantic dreams. Now she would never think of him in the same way again, and when he came to take the children home that evening, she felt bereft, for now she could not even admire him from afar without disturbing thoughts creeping in and spoiling everything. How annoying it was to have to grow up!

Patrick, unaware of the loss of his ardent admirer, was as charming as usual, and Beth asked after Mrs Brontë and the new baby with genuine concern, but she was glad she did not have to go home with him to supervise the putting to bed of four young children and a new-born baby. In the dainty solitude of her bedroom that evening, Beth brushed her hair and was glad she was herself and not dear Maria — even though the latter seemed to be contented with her lot.

★ ★ ★

Two years passed, and the families continued their social calls. Beth often entertained the little ones to tea, and found them good and well-behaved children, independent in many ways as youngsters who are thrown together a good deal and have to amuse each other often are. Maria was still the 'little mother', taking the place of poor Mrs Brontë (who had had yet another baby, Anne, born in January 1820) whose health was never good. Beth was genuinely sorry for her, and did what she could to help, taking the children off their mother's hands as much as she could.

She had discovered by now that Mr Brontë, fond though he was of his family, did not really like young children and found them hard to understand. He treated them as though they were miniature adults, and the result was that they were a curious mixture of childishness and precocity. Even the babies quickly learned not to disturb Papa when he was working in the parlour — all except little Anne, who was, of course, too young yet to comprehend what was required of her.

But grave, quiet Maria, with her long fair hair; and shy Elizabeth, like a tiny copy of her elder sister; plain little Charlotte; Branwell with his carroty hair and jutting nose, and Emily Jane, who was prettiest of all the girls, would come and sit and amuse themselves, speaking docilely when

Beth spoke to them, accepting their tea with manners that were so gravely correct they were almost laughable. Beth encouraged them to be naughty, but it was almost as if they did not know how to romp like other children. They would look at each other, then, as temptation crept in, slowly begin to join her in a game until at last all were shouting with laughter, and flushed with glee. Then Branwell would become boisterous, and Beth would realize that of course they were just ordinary children under the extreme cloaks of discipline imposed by their father. She loved them and looked forward to watching them grow up, to see how they would develop, but this was not to be, for in the April following Anne's birth, the Brontë family moved once more. Beth wrote unemotionally in her diary:

'Took leave of Mr Brontë before leaving home.'

Yes, the family of Patrick and Maria, augmented by the members who had been born at the house in Market Street, was leaving Thornton. Mr Brontë had been appointed perpetual curate to the Parish of St Michael and All Angels at Haworth, eight miles from Thornton, four miles from the town of Keighley, ten miles from the city of Bradford, cut off from them all by high rolling moorland. It was a wild place where the people, with true Yorkshire grit, were a law unto themselves. In fact, Mr Brontë had had a rival for the curacy, a Mr Redhead, but the residents quickly drove him out of the village, leaving the parsonage free for Mr Brontë, who, on 20th April, 1820, moved out from Thornton with his family in a covered wagon, with their household goods following behind in seven carts.

What an adventure! It was the first long journey the children had ever undertaken, and, huddled together in the wagon, they were wild with excitement beneath their unnatural poise as miracles unfolded before their eyes and the carts creaked onwards. Little Emily stared out solemnly at the scenery on the moorland road to Haworth, while, when they came to the village itself and saw the hillside upon which the houses were built, Branwell gazed with interest at the little inn called the Black Bull which stood near the churchyard at the top of the long, steep main street, and Anne's baby eyes crept wonderingly over the dark mass of the church where her father was to preach, surrounded as it was by the graveyard with its sprawling, crowded tombstones that pushed themselves almost into the little oblong of garden that fronted the house — their house — The Parsonage, Haworth, long and low, built of grey stone.

Disdaining the help of an outstretched hand from one of the grown-ups, little Emily Jane Brontë struggled on her small legs to climb the front doorstep, and entered her new home — and, though she did not know it, the world which was to be her kingdom.

2

Emily was six years old when she first experienced the powerful, the terrifying, the dark side, of nature. Already, she had responded eagerly to the wildness and beauty of the moors, and loved her new home dearly, but on 2 September, 1824, she stood with Branwell and Anne and Nancy and Sarah Garrs, the two loyal servants who had come with the family from Thornton and watched something that stirred her blood to the very marrow of her bones, exciting and thrilling her beyond anything she had previously experienced in her short life.

They were all out on the moors, when the air began to darken, the clouds to gather menacingly and the earth to crouch into a watchful stillness. Then, with a shudder that could be felt underfoot, the storm broke, the earth heaved and roared and the ground began to tremble and thrust itself upwards, pouring soil, rocks and boulders down from the hills into the valleys.

This was the Crow Hill bog burst, but all who saw it had no hesitation in referring to it as an earthquake, and Mr Brontë, standing at the back window of the Parsonage, was terrified for the fate of his children. They had been rushed into shelter as soon as the storm began, in spite of the protests of Emily, who was delighted at the violence of the elements, and wanted to stay outdoors and watch. From behind the shelter of a friendly farm-house window, she saw it all, and her soul seemed to fly out and mingle with the wild fury of the storm. It was something she never forgot, one of the most vivid memories of her childhood — more vivid than all the momentous things that had happened to the family since they came to Haworth, and the Glebe House, as the Parsonage was called.

Already there had been great changes since the day she clambered up the front doorstep on legs that were too small to reach where she was going. She heard about them from the others later, but she could never remember them with any accuracy. The family had settled in admirably — Papa, said Maria to her sisters later, was very pleased and happy. Indeed, he wrote:

'*This living is what is called here a Benefice, or Perpetual Curacy. It is mine for life, no one can take it from me . . . my salary is not large, it is only about £200 a year. In addition, I have a good House, which is mine for life, also, and is rent free.'*

Maria told the little ones how famous the pulpit in Haworth Church was, though they did not understand who she meant when she referred to William Grimshaw.

'This used to be his church, once,' she said impressively.

'But who was he?' asked Charlotte.

'A very great preacher. This was the centre of the great Wesleyan revival, and the Wesley brothers preached here, too,' went on Maria, her eyes alight. 'Everybody repented and turned to God. It was wonderful. Papa is following in very famous footsteps.'

Maria understood her father's pride that his journey from a rough cabin in the depths of Ireland should have ended here, in one of the foremost religious centres of Yorkshire, but it meant little to the younger ones, who were far more interested in the wonders they found as they explored the house, shouting to each other at every new discovery. There were currant bushes and lilac, and a central plot of grass in the garden, where Branwell could roll and tumble all he liked, and the little girls could run and skip and hop in freedom. And — most miraculous of all to Emily — was the dovecote in the yard behind the house, where all day the sound of doves cooing and the flutter of white wings could be heard. Emily stood and stared in wonder when she first saw it. Even then, aged less than two years, she had her first glimpse of what was to prove the strongest force in her life, her affinity with nature and the wild things she was to love so dearly.

While Mrs Brontë went about her duties in the neat Georgian house, moving — albeit rather slowly because of her poor health — from the family sitting-room, the parlour on the left of the front door, to oversee the dusting of the room on the right, which Patrick had grandly appropriated as his 'study', the two smaller children, Emily and Anne, remained in the kitchen at the back of the house under the watchful eye of Nancy and Sarah Garrs.

The store-room behind the kitchen was a place of mystery to little Emily, but when the elder children returned from walks on the moors which stretched at the rear of the house, shepherded by their father, she found they brought with them even greater treasure than that which could be found in the store-room. Fallen feathers from the wild moorland birds, bits of rock, flowers or heath, wool from the moorland sheep. Emily fingered such treasures as though they were priceless. All the children loved the moors, but to Emily, the promise of what she would find when she was allowed to join in their walks was infinite.

'When can I come, Papa?' she demanded eagerly.

'When your legs are a bit longer,' he answered, and lifted her in his arms, taking her along the lane to the stile, letting her perch there and look out across the footpath leading to that still-promised land.

'Will my legs be long enough tomorrow?' she asked, and he laughed.

'We'll see, we'll see.'

She willed her legs to grow overnight so that she could go out and see the wonders the others spoke of — the purple heather, the streams and waterfalls, the great rolling expanse of fold upon fold of empty moorland that was yet full of things to see, if you knew where to look.

Emily was a precocious child, as all the children were precocious. Her father treated them — as Beth Firth had observed — like miniature adults. Maria, the eldest, was almost a little woman at six years old, and all the children had started to learn to read and write, even Emily, who, determined not to be left out, covered pages with her scribbles which to her were magic script. Only baby

Anne still cooed and gurgled at her infant's toys, too young yet to join in the activities of the others.

Everything seemed set for a happy — if frugal — future, but it was not to be. His wife tried to hide her continued frailty from Patrick, but the time came when she could no longer conceal the fact that she was very ill. When her illness was diagnosed as an incurable cancer of the stomach, it was as if a lightning bolt had descended from heaven to shatter Patrick's life, for she became ill in the January after they removed to Haworth, and suffered a long-drawn-out agony which ended mercifully with her death on 25th September, 1821.

Once their mother had taken to the sick-bed from which she was never to rise, the children were thrown more and more upon themselves, for Patrick devoted all the attention he could spare from his duties to his wife. They clung together, six little creatures left to fend for themselves, and now Emily had her wish to walk on the moors, for they all — except baby Anne — walked out hand in hand with Maria and Elizabeth watching over their little 'family' like small mother-hens over a brood of chicks. They knew their mother was ill upstairs, and were quiet and docile when in the house, with that unspoken apprehension that children feel in the presence of serious illness from which they are excluded.

Mrs Brontë did not ask to see them. Probably she felt it would disturb them to see her pain. So while her husband devotedly waited on her — he would allow no one but himself to nurse her during the long, agonized nights — the children ate their meals quietly in the kitchen, or wandered out on the moor, or sat playing together in the little room over the stairs that was called 'the children's study'.

'Why must we be quiet all the time?' Branwell asked belligerently one day, and Maria was there at once, her finger laid across his lips.

'Because Mama is sick — you know that, and we would disturb her.'

'But she's been sick for such a long time,' protested Branwell. 'When will she get better, Maria? I want to show her my new top and whip.'

'I don't know, but you can show them to her when she's better,' Maria reassured him.

'I want her to come out with us — I want to show her the moors,' said Emily, to whom the open moorland had been a revelation. 'When she's better, will she come out on

29

the moors with us, Maria?'

'Yes, probably, but now she is very poorly, and we must play quietly and let her sleep,' said the little mother gravely.

They had never been particularly sturdy children, and the Parsonage at Haworth was often cold, with its stone floors and lack of carpets and curtains. They could not afford carpets, and because he and nearly all the children were short-sighted and likely to knock over a candle, or have some similar sort of accident, Patrick would allow no curtains as he had an obsessive fear of fire. The result was that in summer, when it was hot outside, the house was deliciously cool, but during the months of the long Yorkshire winter, when the wind howled down the moors and buffeted the stone walls, and the snow piled high round the yard and garden — the sort of winters they were to come to know well — the children felt the cold bitterly, and it was rare that one or other of them was not ill with a cough or a cold or some other childish ailment.

As Mrs Brontë grew worse, Patrick felt that nothing could add to his burden, but he was wrong. All six of the children fell victim to scarlet fever, and while they lay racked and gasping, their mother quietly slipped away, leaving the head of the house distraught, bereaved and helpless. His wife's last words had been:

'My poor children, my poor children — '

And when they recovered their health and spirits, as inevitably they did, and accepted with equanimity Patrick's news that their Mama was now with Jesus, who was to comfort the poor sorrowing widower? Patrick wrote painfully to an acquaintance:

'And when my dear wife was dead and buried and gone, and when I missed her at every corner and when her memory was hourly raised by the innocent yet distressing prattle of my children, I do assure you my dear Sir, from what I felt, I was happy at the recollection that to sorrow, not as those without hope, was no sin; that our Lord himself had wept over his departed friend — .'

Patrick himself suffered from bronchial trouble, and had done so for a long time, though he was a hardy and enthusiastic walker on the moors. He had taken to muffling his throat and chest with a scarf over the points of his high collar, a habit he never dropped all his life. Now, he felt all the more deeply concerned, with his wife gone, about the health and fortunes of his children and himself. They must be encouraged to eat as much good food as they could, and to wear flannel to keep them warm, while he must take extra care of himself, for they depended on him for everything, including the roof over their heads. If — God forbid! — he should die too, the children would have to leave the house and be rendered homeless, a prospect he could not contemplate. So he must raise them to be aware that, should anything happen to him, they would be driven to earning their own living. They must be educated, as well as he could afford with his limited means — plans came and went in his mind.

But once the hurt of his wife's loss had lost its immediacy, Patrick was able to take better stock of his position. At present, the house and children were being looked after by a newcomer to the family circle, Miss Elizabeth Branwell, Maria Brontë's unmarried sister, who had made the long journey from Penzance by coach in order to help nurse Maria in her desperate illness, and to take charge of the children. It was to have been a temporary measure only, and when Maria died, Miss Branwell — or Aunt Branwell, as the children called her with something approaching awe, for there was an air that was slightly forbidding about the maiden lady — had every expectation that Patrick would marry again and that she would be free to return to her quiet and genteel life in Cornwall.

Patrick himself saw that his children needed a mother, and the result was that — after a decent interval — he made three proposals, one of them, by an odd twist of fate, to Beth Firth at Thornton. The young girl who had worshipped him from afar had now matured, however, and gently rejected his proposal, while the other ladies to whom he proposed also replied in the negative. So Patrick gave up any idea of a further marriage, and Miss Branwell stayed on at the Parsonage to oversee to the household and bring up the children. She really had no choice if she was to do her duty, and to Miss Branwell, 'doing one's duty' was the greatest thing that mattered in life. She did her best to instil this code of living into the children, and succeeded in varying degrees.

The children had been driven into a close single unit by their mother's long illness and death, and were remarkably interdependent on each other. Small Maria and Elizabeth had taken Mama's place now, far more than Aunt Branwell was ever able to do. They respected her, they deferred to her, but they did not love her. And as for Emily, she had already begun to cultivate the aloofness that was to be the hallmark of her character in later years, and when Aunt scolded, and Charlotte seethed and Anne cried, Emily simply retreated quietly into herself.

As the years slipped by, Aunt Branwell settled the household into a routine, and tried to teach the girls the rudiments of sewing, reading, discussing the current affairs and politics of the day, and all the things they would need to know in order to run a household when they had one of their own. It was obvious by now that here was a family of remarkable children. Maria, the eldest, was brilliant, and Patrick soon realized that his elder daughters had passed the limits of what their Aunt could teach them, and should be sent away to school.

So off went Maria and Elizabeth to the expensive Crofton House School near Wakefield, but Patrick, with his limited means, soon had to withdraw them, and lighted upon a solution to the problem of his children's education that seemed indeed to have been sent from heaven.

In January 1924, the Clergy Daughters' School opened its doors at Cowan Bridge near Kirkby Lonsdale, about fifty miles from Haworth. This was partly a charitable institution, which meant that board and education could be offered to the daughters of poor clergymen at a nominal fee of £14 per annum, the rest of the cost being met by the donations of its sponsors. The girls, according to the prospectus, were not only to be given an excellent education, including music and languages, but were to be fitted for future roles as governesses, one of the few professions by which a young lady could earn a living in those days.

It seemed like an answer to prayer. Patrick and Aunt Branwell discussed the matter thoroughly, and came to the same conclusion — that it would be foolish not to take advantage of such a remarkable scheme. So in 1824, all the girls except Anne departed for Cowan Bridge.

They had all had whooping-cough in the spring, and in July, when Maria and Elizabeth were taken to the school by their Papa, the weakness after their illness had still not quite left them, so that they were frail and pale. Maria, particularly, was eager to learn, to expand her mind, to wander in the uncharted regions of her yet unexplored intellect. Maria was then ten and a half, and Elizabeth nine years old, but they were far in advance of other girls of their age with regard to maturity, and before she left home, Maria used to discuss the affairs of the day with her Papa with all the aplomb of a mature adult.

Admittedly, there were tears when Maria and Elizabeth departed, for since their Mama's death, Charlotte and Branwell in particular had come to look on Maria as a second mother.

'I don't want you to go,' said Charlotte, red-faced, clinging to her sister, and Maria gently disengaged her hands.

'But Charlotte darling, soon you'll be coming too, and Emily.'

'And then we'll all be together? For ever and ever?' demanded Charlotte.

'Of course we will,' said Maria, and gave her sister a kiss. 'And just think of all the wonderful things we'll learn — French and geography and history.'

So Charlotte stood bravely and waved as Papa departed with his two eldest daughters. A month later, she followed them to Cowan Bridge, leaving Emily, still recovering from her illness, to join them in November. Anne was still too little to go to school, and Papa had decided to teach Branwell himself.

Before Emily set off to school, however, she had experienced the Crow Hill bog burst, and had also seen changes in the household. Nancy and Sarah Garrs left the service of the Brontës — Nancy to be married — and they were replaced by an elderly woman, Tabitha Aykroyd, who immediately took Emily, as well as baby Anne and the unpredictable Branwell, to her rough but affectionate heart. 'Tabby', as she was to become to the family in later years, was loved by all the children in due course, but Emily was the one who knew her first, and was first to experience her Yorkshire ways, her dialect stories and her combination of stern Methodist principles mingled with a weakness for gossip about the people of the district and her habit of telling horrific and dubious tales of violent and supernatural happenings.

On November 25th, 1824, Emily set off on her second great adventure. She travelled the fifty miles to school in the charge of the guard on the coach from Keighley, a small girl of six, with dark brown curls under her bonnet, wide eyes that seemed to be weighing everything up, and a quaint poise for one so young. She was, in fact, the youngest pupil at the school, and when she arrived there, it was recorded that she 'Reads very prettily and works a little'. But being the youngest, she became the darling of the whole school and was petted by all; and being of a naturally independent disposition, she took it as her due, and went about the little tasks she was set without taking much notice of anything else that was happening around her.

This was fortunate, for the elder girls,

especially Charlotte, were suffering rebelliously from harsh rules, iron discipline designed to make the pupils meek and humble in their stations in life, and general treatment with regard to food and clothing and concern for their health which, according to Charlotte's later description of the school given under a different name in *Jane Eyre*, was hardly fit for a dog and certainly not for growing children. The institution described so optimistically in the prospectus, where Papa had confidently entrusted his daughters, was in fact badly managed, badly run, and the pupils were callously and indifferently treated, given food they could not eat, were constantly cold throughout the long winter, and the majority of them suffered colds, coughs and other illnesses as the site of the school itself, combined with neglect, was such that it encouraged the spread of infection.

In the spring, an epidemic of typhoid fever broke out, and Emily, at six, played happily amid the general misery and discontent, and was unaffected by it. In February, something happened which momentarily shocked her out of her little shell of unconcern. She came across Charlotte in a corner, tears stealing down her sister's thin cheeks, sunken after the ordeals of the winter.

'Have you hurt yourself, Charlotte? Why

are you crying?' she asked.

'I'm not crying. You know I never cry,' choked Charlotte, digging her fists into her eyes.

Emily waited patiently while her sister struggled to control herself. It was true that she never cried. Fiercely rebellious and proud, her rage showed itself in outbursts of temper or sullen silences, but what had happened was too much for her, in her weakened condition, to control, for her concern was for someone else, not for herself.

'I'll never forgive them, never,' she managed, at last.

'Forgive who?' questioned Emily.

'Them. Everybody. They've hurt Maria over and over, and called her untidy, and punished her for *nothing*,' said Charlotte, in a voice that trembled with defensive pride. 'They've humiliated her and picked on her and — her cough — nobody took any notice of it, and it got worse and worse, and now — oh, Emily, she's ill.'

'We were all ill before we came,' pointed out Emily, logically. 'I had measles and whooping-cough, but I'm better now.'

'But she's *very* ill. So bad,' said Charlotte, choking again, 'that they've sent for Papa to take her home.'

Emily's mouth fell into an 'o' of surprise

as she considered this.

'Will she die?' she asked at last, 'like Mama?' She could hardly remember their Mama, and while Maria had mothered the older children, she and Anne had spent most of their time with Nancy and Sarah Garrs, so she was not as attached to Maria as Charlotte and Branwell, nor as dependent on her emotionally.

Charlotte turned stricken eyes on her.

'Oh, no, no, not Maria,' she whispered piteously. 'Please God, not Maria.'

But in fact, Maria did die, at home in the Parsonage, aged eleven, on 6th May. She was quickly followed by Elizabeth, who was sent home on the last day of May, in a state of advanced consumption, as her sister had been, and who lingered only two weeks before she too joined Maria in death. She was ten years old.

Patrick, who had had no idea of the state of things at the school, was so alarmed by Maria's death and Elizabeth's condition when she arrived home that he set out immediately to remove Charlotte and Emily, and on 1st June, 1825, the little girls left Cowan Bridge never to return. Whereas the experience had hardly affected small Emily, it had marked Charlotte for the rest of her life, and she never did forgive or forget. She took her revenge years later when 'Lowood School' figured in her book *Jane Eyre*, and she was able to exorcise her pent-up feelings of outrage and pain and mortified pride, and to recollect with icy vitriol in her pen the treatment that had killed her dearly loved sisters.

While Emily was still at school, unaware of Maria's suffering at home, Branwell too was being scarred to the very soul by watching at Maria's death-bed. His eldest sister had become a second mother to him as well as Charlotte, and it was as though he was losing his Mama all over again. Most terrible of all was the ordeal, which was customary at the time, of saying goodbye to the dead. Branwell had in him a mingled streak of fascination and horror with the morbid, and while Emily, with her clear-sightedness, could accept a fact like death with equanimity, to Branwell it became something much more momentous. When all was over, he was a terrified child as he leaned over Maria's open coffin to kiss the marble-cold cheek, and her serene face as she lay there, and the thought of her being lowered into the black, unfathomable depths of the grave, haunted him for the rest of his life.

When Charlotte and Emily returned from Cowan Bridge, he told them about it, and though he could not express exactly what he felt, he described visions that were fanciful and ghoulish. Emily, to whom everything was rather bewildering at present, listened with the rapt attention of the six-year-old to her big brother, who all of a sudden seemed much older and certainly much bossier than she remembered.

'I was with her when she died,' declared Branwell, in hollow tones. 'I watched her die. And I saw them bury her.'

'All dead people have to be buried,' said Emily, sensibly.

'Yes, but she doesn't rest in her grave, you know. Listen tonight,' urged Branwell, and Charlotte and Emily were too young to notice the desperate bravado that lurked at the back of his voice. 'She moans round the windows, calling 'Let me in, let me in'.'

Charlotte shuddered.

'Oh, Branwell, don't be silly, of course she doesn't. She's at peace now, and with God.'

Emily said nothing, but a seed had sunk deep into her mind, and was to grow there and germinate until, years later, Maria became the ghost of Catherine Earnshaw wailing at the window of Wuthering Heights, chilling and terrifying. The chill was Branwell's fear at Maria's death, and the terror was his too, that of a child faced with the unknown and the unfathomable. Even in death, Maria still retained an influence on the brother and sisters she had left behind her.

3

'Emily — you can't! Oh, Emily, please come down!'

Anne's wail of dismay echoed throughout the Parsonage garden, but Branwell turned to her scornfully.

'At least she's got guts,' he had to admit, for he would have much preferred to play the part of Prince Charles escaping in the oak tree, but as Emily was growing fast and was now taller than he was, to Emily had fallen the honour of celebrating this particular Oak Apple Day by climbing the double cherry-tree outside Papa's window and hiding in the mass of blossom. There was no oak tree in the garden, so a cherry had to do.

With a flurry of skirts, Emily disappeared into the foaming flowery mass, and the others took up their roles of soldiers hunting for the royal fugitive. This was one of the rare days when they could enjoy their make-believe dramas out of doors in peace, for Papa was off on his parish duties, and Aunt Branwell had set out on her favourite occupation, though she indulged in it only rarely — to make social calls.

'Where does the villain hide? I see him not,' declaimed Branwell, a hand to his brow as he peered round the sunny garden.

'There is no sign of him,' agreed Charlotte, 'but he cannot have escaped. Our men are tireless in their vigilance.'

'He will be caught, and then — ha! — we shall see whether he behaves like a man of royal blood or a craven coward,' Branwell laughed harshly.

There was a sudden loud crack from the cherry tree which made them all jump, and Emily's voice crying, 'Oh!'

'What's happening?' demanded Charlotte, forgetting the game.

'The branch — it's breaking,' came Emily's voice, 'look out!'

And a violent shaking of the cherry blossom preceded a thud as the branch on which the hunted king had been sitting came away from the tree and fell to the ground. Emily managed to jump clear, and landed amid a tangle of her long skirts, unhurt except for a bruise or two, which she pooh-poohed, but Branwell was staring in dismay at the tree. It was Papa's favourite, and now, a great white gash marred the lovely shape of it where the branch had broken away.

'What will Papa say?' whispered Anne,

frightened by the enormity of what they had done.

'We'll ask Tabby what to do,' decided Charlotte, after a moment.

Tabby was called out from the kitchen to see the damage, and she shook her head, but came up with a suggestion that at once solved the problem.

'Of course — a bag of soot from John Brown the stonemason's yard. That'll hide the mark,' exclaimed Branwell. 'I'll fetch it.'

Tabby departed once more for the kitchen, complaining loudly about the escapades of 'yon childer', while the 'childer' in question smeared soot over the white mark on the tree. When they had finished, they looked at each other. Papa would never guess what had happened.

But all the same, when he came home in the evening, the children could not hide their guilt, and told him about the accident to the tree. He sternly made them promise not to do such a thing again — but there was a smile trembling on his lips as, one by one, the dejected little group trailed out of his study.

★ ★ ★

After the deaths of Maria and Elizabeth, all the children remained together at home, where Emily grew up in an atmosphere that was greatly influenced by the precocity of her older brother and sister. Aunt Branwell continued to teach the girls such subjects as housewifery, needlework and her own brand of religion, and Papa encouraged them to read widely, and joined them in debates on politics and subjects of the day, but most important of all to Emily was the influence of the moors and that of the secret world the children created for themselves.

Stories had always played a large part in their lives. When Maria was alive, she had read aloud to them, and now that they could read themselves, they availed themselves of any and every sort of literature that came their way — for Papa laid no limits on what they were allowed to read — and at first acted out their little stories themselves. In this, they were encouraged by Patrick, who described later how they banded themselves together into a sort of secret society and drew on their own resources to construct what they always called their 'plays'.

'When mere children,' he recalled, 'Charlotte and her brother and sisters used to invent and act little plays of their own in which the Duke of Wellington was sure to come off conqueror. When a dispute would not infrequently arise amongst them regarding the comparative merits of him, Bonaparte, Hannibal and Caesar. When the argument rose to its height, I had sometimes to come in and settle the dispute to the best of my judgement.

'Sometimes they also wrote little works of fiction they called miniature novels. Charlotte got her knowledge of the Duke of Wellington from the newspapers and from what she heard in company and other heroes from Ancient History.'

So Patrick was aware that from acting out their plays, the children had turned to writing, but he was never fully to know the intensity with which all four children lived in their make-believe world. It was created early in Emily's life, and became, as they grew, a substitute for reality, a fantasy world into which they could all withdraw at will and dream about during the day. It became to all of them a great source of comfort in times that were not always easy, but they did not recognise its dangers. Living in his 'infernal world' as an adult drove Branwell insane; while Charlotte, with a great deal of heartbreak, managed to free herself in later years from its clinging grasp; and even Anne was affected in some lesser degree.

To Emily, it was something much more important. Sensible, practical, realistic in many ways, she was to completely reject actual life in favour of an existence that was poetic and passionate and lived at an extremely high level of imagination, but all this was to come later. In their childhood, the creation that would affect them all like a drug, began simply enough, and perhaps naturally, it was the older children, Charlotte and Branwell, who led the way.

Since the deaths of Maria and Elizabeth, Charlotte had taken on the responsibility of 'little mother' to the younger ones, and one of her earliest pieces of writing was a present for her youngest sister, written when she was about twelve, a sort of fairy-tale that began: 'There was once a little girl and her name was Ane — .'

Such tales were outside the scope of their 'plays', and ordinary storytelling did not enter into the creation of the secret worlds that first found expression when Emily was nearly eight years old, for as well as writing down tiny books and manuscripts about the scenes and places they created, the children also acted out these same mysterious worlds which they could all share, in real life, making themselves participants, under various pseudonyms, in the game.

Charlotte recorded in her tiny volume: *The History of the Year 1829* both the reality of the domestic scene around her in the Parsonage kitchen, and the imaginary worlds they had created themselves, showing just how real their 'plays' were in comparison with their ordinary day-to-day happenings. She wrote:

'While I write this, I am in the kitchen of the Parsonage, Haworth; Tabby, the servant, is washing up the breakfast things, and Anne, my youngest sister (Maria was my eldest) is kneeling on a chair, looking at some cakes which Tabby had been baking for us. Emily is in the parlour, brushing the carpet. Papa and Branwell are gone to Keighley. Aunt is upstairs in her room, and I am sitting by the table writing this in the kitchen ... Our plays were established; 'Young Men', June, 1826; 'Our Fellows', July 1827; 'Islanders', December, 1827. These are our three great plays, that are not kept secret ... The 'Young Men's' play took its rise from some wooden soldiers Branwell had; 'Our Fellows' from 'Aesop's Fables'; and the 'Islanders' from several events which happened.'

50

As the creation of these 'plays' had formed such a traumatic event in all the children's lives, it is interesting to look more closely at this little extract from Charlotte's book before finding out more about the 'plays' themselves. From her description of the kitchen scene, it is obvious that life at the Parsonage was both busy and happy. Obviously by this time, the family had acquired a carpet, as Emily was busy brushing it — she, even at her early age, was beginning to turn into a very useful and competent housewife, though no doubt she day-dreamed while she was doing such mundane tasks as carpet-brushing, both about her beloved moors, and how she would go out of doors with the others in the afternoon and wander in glorious freedom and isolation, as well as about her contribution to the various 'plays'. Even though they could not write as well as the older ones, the younger children were not excluded from the game, but would tell Charlotte their ideas and she would write them down.

★ ★ ★

It was just before Emily's eighth birthday when the 'play' *Young Men* innocently began. The children were all in bed when Papa arrived home late from Leeds. He had brought gifts for them, but it was not until the next morning that they found out what the gifts were. Perhaps there were boxes of bon-bons for the girls — for Papa would not have forgotten them — but the pièce de resistance was Branwell's present, and he came dashing upstairs with it. A box of toy soldiers! Emily and Charlotte jumped out of bed and immediately seized one each in their hands.

'This is the Duke of Wellington!' cried Charlotte. 'He's mine, and he's the Duke!'

And she gazed rapturously at the little painted figure, convinced that it was the best-looking and the tallest of all the twelve.

Emily deliberated before making her choice, then she too picked up one of the soldiers, and said, 'This one is mine.'

'He's just like you, such a grave little thing. I name him 'Gravey',' said Charlotte, and Branwell laughed.

Anne was given a choice when she appeared from the room where she slept with her Aunt, and she picked out one that the irrepressible Charlotte christened 'Waiting-Boy', while Branwell, important in his ownership of the whole boxful, took up a figure that he decided should represent Bonaparte. He told the girls with gracious condescension that they might play with the soldiers, though they mustn't forget that all really belonged to him.

And straight away, the game began. The wooden soldiers were transformed into young men, and proceeded to found a kingdom on the African coast that boasted Charlotte's Duke of Wellington as its king. They built a city which was called Great Glass Town, or Glasstown, and the Twelves, as the Young Men were called, set about various adventures and activities which were faithfully recorded by Charlotte and Branwell. In all their doings, they were assisted by four Chief Genii named Tallii, Branii, Emmii and Annii — who else but Charlotte, Branwell, Emily and Anne, in the guise of all-magic, all-powerful beings who appeared at crucial moments, sometimes in clouds of smoke and awe-inspiring majesty, and who could do everything, including bringing back some dead hero to life?

Their imaginations wandered far beyond the four walls of the modest Parsonage, and Charlotte could revel in the exotic extravagance she loved as much as she liked, while Emily's contributions — though verbal only at this time, for she was not able to write the chronicles that her eldest sister produced with such ease, revealed a dry sense of humour and an observation of setting and background that was to be found in all her work, based on her own experiences in the village around her. All the magic, the glamour that Charlotte loved was not for her — she was far more practical and her contributions were down-to-earth and full of common-sense. Branwell became carried away by tales of blood and gore, and even Anne made her small contribution, though she was too young as yet to take a full part in the exciting unfolding of the Glasstown Chronicles.

The little books that Charlotte and Branwell produced were originally intended to be written, published and sold by the Twelves themselves, and so, as the soldiers were small, the volumes were correspondingly tiny, usually measuring about two inches by one-and-a-half inches, written on scraps of paper and with covers made from wrapping-paper, the whole printed in a microscopic script that was almost impossible for an adult to read without the aid of a magnifying glass. The little volumes were sewn neatly together, some were a fraction larger, and most had decorative title-pages just like a real book. They began with perhaps four pages in each, but gradually, the amount of pages increased, until some of the minute books contained up to twenty thousand words.

Charlotte in particular was in her element, while Branwell wrote so fast and furiously that, though he was considered as a boy to be brilliant, and the hope of the family rested on him as far as doing 'great things' went, he had in fact written himself out in these miniature volumes by the time he grew to adulthood.

There were stories, novels, histories and dramas — anything and everything that they read or which happened in the real world somehow found its way into the chronicles of Glasstown. They 'published' tiny magazines and newspapers, all of which were supposed to be written by the Glasstown inhabitants themselves, but which were of course all written by Charlotte and Branwell under various pseudonyms. There were reviews and letters, volumes of poetry, comments on current affairs. All told, it was a prodigious feat, and because of the microscopic nature of the script, the 'secret Plays', which, Charlotte wrote, were so much more interesting than the ones that were not kept secret, managed to retain their secret for over a century, and this 'web of sunny air' which they wove in childhood (and about which Charlotte wrote one of her best-known poems) remained known to none but its creators.

Emily did not contribute, apart from verbally, to this great output of literature, and neither did Anne, although the two were kindly included, in their roles of Genii, whenever the Genii appeared, bringing up the rear while the more active Genii got on with the business in hand, but Emily, who shared a bed with Charlotte, did make suggestions, particularly observations on nature, which her sister included in the Glasstown chronicles, and she added one feature of the 'plays' which was to remain permanently her own.

While the girls were supposed to be sleeping innocently, they were in fact discussing various aspects of the unfolding of the story.

'There's a Palace of Instruction,' whispered Emily, carried away with enthusiasm.

'What's that?' asked Charlotte.

'It's a sort of college, on an island in the Atlantic,' Emily went on. 'It has a thousand pupils there, all drawn from the best families in the land. And it has great vaulted cells and dungeons deep under the earth, where the children are sent when they're naughty. They scream and scream as much as they like, but nobody can hear them.'

Emily, clearly, found the vault-like cellars of Haworth Parsonage a great inspiration to her imagination!

She also discovered two other stimuli which were to influence her writing in future years. One was the 'idea' of Scotland, which she

56

never visited. This came from various sources in her reading, and the picture of wild lakes and rugged seascapes, added to a landscape not unlike her beloved moors, appealed to her immensely. The family was allowed to see the popular *Blackwood's Magazine*, which they could not afford to buy, through the generosity of the local doctor, and they devoured it eagerly, especially the work of James Hogg, a Scottish shepherd whose writing on all things Scottish made Emily feel she knew the country as well as she knew the area around her own home.

In addition, Emily broke away early from the tradition which Charlotte and Anne, in common with most young ladies of the day, believed in implicitly. They regarded men as superior beings, and thought women should give way to them in everything. Emily turned up her nose at this idea, her inspiration stemming partly from her own nature — for she knew her worth — and partly from the example of the Princess Victoria, heir to the English throne, who, as a future Queen, would reign supreme over bowing and deferential men. The picture of a woman — moreover, a mere girl who was in fact only a few months younger than Emily herself — being raised to such a position of authority and regality shed a spell over

Emily's mind, and much of the work she produced later was concerned with Queens and Princesses as her main characters, rather than all-conquering male heroes.

In 1830, when Emily was twelve, Patrick became seriously ill with congestion of the lungs, but fortunately recovered. The illness had stirred up, however, his ever-present worry about his children's future if anything should happen to him, and anxiety swept over him like a great wave.

Aunt was sitting with him as he convalesced after his illness, and he began to talk about the situation.

'Branwell will do all right — he's a boy, and a young man can always make his way in the world,' he said, his voice still hoarse from his lung trouble. He fingered the scarf he still wound round his neck and chest. 'But the girls — .'

'The girls need to be educated properly, that's true. They'll have a living to earn,' agreed Aunt Branwell, her head bent over her sewing. 'I suppose they will have to become governesses, or something of the sort,' and she shook her head, for to any well-bred gentlewoman such as herself, governesses belonged to the lower ranks of society.

'They should go to school,' murmured Patrick, lost in thought, and Aunt looked up from her sewing, anxiety in her eyes.

'Remember what happened the last time.'

'Yes, but this will be different. They're older now — but it's a question of finding the money,' said Patrick, almost to himself.

He did not like to ask Aunt Branwell for money, though she possessed a little of her own, enough to give her a modest income, and feeling the pressure of trouble heavy upon him, he wrote to Beth Firth, who was now a married woman, but who had remained on friendly terms with the family even after her rejection of Patrick's proposal and her marriage to the vicar of Huddersfield.

She consulted Charlotte's god-parents, the Reverend and Mrs Atkinson, who were old friends of Patrick's from the Thornton days, and the childless couple were only too happy to assist with the education of their god-daughter. They offered to finance Charlotte at a school at Roe Head, near Dewsbury, about twenty miles from Haworth, which was personally known to them and was new and very select. It was the Misses Woolers' academy for young ladies, which was the complete opposite in all ways from the Clergy Daughters' School at Cowan Bridge, and there, Papa informed Charlotte, she was to go.

'Go to school, Papa? Me?' exclaimed Charlotte in dismay when he told her. 'But — oh, remember what happened at the other school. I shall hate it.'

'This is a very different proposition altogether,' said Papa, while Charlotte and Branwell exchanged agonized looks, for they were deep in the creation of their secret world. Emily and Anne looked on in interested silence.

'You girls will all need to be able to earn your own livings, and a good education is very necessary if you are to become governesses or teachers,' Papa went on severely. 'I should have thought that you, Charlotte, would have been grateful to the Atkinsons for giving you this chance.'

Charlotte debated with herself.

'Well, of course I'm grateful,' she said slowly, at last. 'It's just that — oh, well, yes, of course I can see that we need to be properly educated.' Suddenly, the thought of learning, of expanding her mind, took over, and she smiled. 'I will write and thank dear Reverend and Mrs Atkinson at once. When shall I be going, Papa?'

Patrick was gratified, and preparations began to send Charlotte off to school, but the prospective new pupil snatched a quiet moment from the whirl of excitement to consult with her fellow-Genii as to what was to happen to their 'play' now that they were to be separated.

They sat in solemn conclave, and Charlotte pronounced in hollow tones:

'This must be the end. The great Glasstown will be no more. I have written a poem to celebrate the event.'

They all joined in the mournful lament.
'No mortal may further the vision reveal;
Human eye may not pierce what a spirit
    would seal.
The secrets of genii my tongue may
    not tell,
But hoarsely they murmured: 'Bright
    city farewell'!'

Charlotte set off to school, half-excited, half-fearful at mixing with strangers, in a covered cart, and the others gathered in a little group to wave goodbye to her. She was off on the long journey of her life, and everything was changed. Branwell was most affected by her departure, for she had been his constant companion in the recording of the Glasstown chronicles, and now not only was she no longer there, but Glasstown itself had been destroyed for ever. Branwell determined to revive the great city,

61

and he continued to write Glasstown news to Charlotte at school, while she in her turn was still wandering in her mind amid the gorgeous palaces and columns, even while she made new friends and settled down in a school which she quickly found stimulated and enriched her mind.

Emily, who was now thirteen, asserted herself for the first time in her life. So far, she had followed where the others led, but now she took command of her own destiny, albeit in a small way.

In between the chronicling of the adventures of the Twelves, the children had had two other main 'plays'. One was a drama called *Our Fellows*, which involved islands where the inhabitants were ten miles tall, and was inspired by *Aesop's Fables*; and the other was called *The Islanders* where each child chose an island and peopled it with famous figures of their own, but neither of these had lasted as long or as intensely as the Glasstown chronicles, and now, with Charlotte gone and Branwell doggedly pursuing Glasstown news, Emily took Anne out on the moors and told her that she had decided to start a 'play' of her own.

Since Charlotte's departure, Emily and Anne had drawn very much closer together. Now they joined forces in creating a new kingdom, Gondal, which was the 'island in the Atlantic' where the Palace of Instruction was situated. They charted their imaginary land, which was fifty miles round, and began to choose heroes and heroines of their own, one of whom was the Princess Victoria, who had made a brief appearance in the chronicles, but whose adventures remained to be followed and invented with enthusiasm.

Emily peopled her island with Emperors and Empresses, with Princes and Princesses, who were for ever being harried by rebel Republican armies, but even more than their characters they found, as they roamed the moors, that the very spirit of the moorland had crept into their invention, and this drew them closer. They became like twins, linked together by their creation, and by a sympathy of mood and thought which made them identify themselves with Gondal so that it became something much more than a game; it became a way of life.

Emily, even as a child, developed a great longing for freedom, and she found this as she wandered the moors with Anne. Freedom to her meant freedom of both body and spirit. Freedom of body was to be found amongst the rocks and heath and bracken that stretched fold upon fold, beautiful in all the changing seasons; and freedom of spirit let her choose as the principal actors in her drama feminine characters who were bold, adventurous and scornful of restrictions on their ardent and passionate natures.

This was the great difference between Emily Jane Brontë and her sisters. Charlotte and Anne grew up influenced by outside promptings — Charlotte by a desire to be beautiful, to be loved, to find a strong man to lean on and revere; Anne was crippled by her Aunt's narrow and unforgiving religious creed, but Emily grew like one of her own heather-bells, a child of nature, essentially herself, and when anything threatened to try and dominate her, she fought it off by whatever means lay in her power.

Her Gondal world sustained her through her mundane household tasks, through the lessons that Aunt tried to teach, and all Aunt's constant bemoaning of the genteel life she had left behind in Cornwall. What did Penzance society mean to Emily when she could walk with Queens and Empresses? What did 'earning her own living' matter against the integrity of following the dictates of her powerful mind? God had given her a light — and she refused to hide it under a bushel and conform. She expressed her feelings in her poetry, for the Gondal saga was full of poetry:

'Riches I hold in light esteem
And Love I laugh to scorn
And lust of Fame was but a dream
That vanished with the morn —

'And if I pray, the only prayer
That moves my lips for me
Is — 'Leave the heart that now I bear
And give me liberty'.'

There were many signs, as the Gondal saga developed and took possession of Emily's mind, that pointed the way towards what she would later incorporate into her great work *Wuthering Heights*. Even as far back as the Glasstown stories, there had been a character who was orphaned and adopted by a kind benefactor, but who was wild, ungrateful and savage, and turned against the man who had befriended him as soon as he was old enough. In the Gondal poems, Emily explored the figure of a mysterious, dark-haired boy or man who was similarly cursed with a wild and unruly nature that he could not help because he had been born with it. Even at that early age, she had begun to ponder on the subject of inherent evil which was to find its fullest outlet in her creation of the person of Heathcliff.

While all this was going on in her

developing mind, outwardly, Emily was just an ordinary girl, the only thing that marked her from her sisters being her great reserve and shyness with strangers. While surrounded by the familiar things of home and the people she loved, she was a stimulating companion, child-like in her sense of mischief and her love of jokes, having learned a robust sense of humour from Tabby. She was devoted to her pets, and there were dogs in the house from quite early days, to whom Emily would whistle whenever she wanted them to accompany her on a walk, in a most unladylike fashion, but then, Emily Brontë was growing up to be a very unusual sort of young lady.

4

The Parsonage was shining like a new pin. From top to bottom, everything was scrubbed and polished, and all the girls were dressed in their best. Charlotte's school friend Miss Ellen Nussey was to pay them a visit, and in their sheltered and quiet lives, this was a great occasion.

Charlotte, now a young woman of seventeen, scurried here and there to make sure that everything was ready for the advent of her friend, for Miss Nussey was a lady, born into society, and when Charlotte had visited her the previous year, after they had both left school, she had found that Ellen's home was a great, battlemented mansion, set gloriously amid gardens and lawns, where life was conducted at a genteel social level of which Aunt (bemoaning the society of Penzance) would certainly have approved.

It had been a pleasant visit, though somewhat disturbing at times for Charlotte, who could not bring herself to accept with equanimity the fact that she was small and plain and socially tongue-tied with strangers. She still longed secretly to be beautiful, elegant and at ease in any situation.

'Has she come?' Charlotte cried suddenly, running out of the house at what she thought was the sound of wheels in the lane outside the Parsonage, but it proved to be a false alarm. Ellen had not arrived yet, and Charlotte returned to the other girls, who were waiting with Aunt in the parlour to welcome their guest.

She looked at them with eyes that were just a fraction anxious. She loved her sisters dearly, but how would they appear to Ellen's more cosmopolitan eye? Fifteen-year-old Emily was now tall, the tallest person in the family except for Papa, and was slender and graceful in her movements. Her dark hair was teased into frizzy curls, and she looked at her best. Charlotte did so hope that Emily would be friendly to Ellen. She could be difficult with strangers at times, and of course, Charlotte herself understood that it was just Emily's reserved, self-reliant nature, but would Ellen see it like that, or gain the wrong impression?

Anne, on the other hand, would behave excellently. She was a little shy, it was true, but that would soon wear off, and she looked very pretty with her long brown curls hanging on her shoulders, her violet-blue eyes and delicate complexion, flushed now as she prepared to welcome her sister's friend.

Charlotte's eyes went next to Aunt. She, as usual, was dressed in a silk dress — a black one — and one of her extravagant mob-caps. The false front of auburn curls that she habitually wore curled over her forehead, and Charlotte felt a sudden pang. Would Ellen think her Aunt just a little eccentric? A little odd? Would she find the Parsonage and life there so very different from her own — ? Her musings were cut short by the unmistakable sound of wheels outside, and, misgivings forgotten, she hurried out to greet her dear Ellen.

Whatever her feelings about this wild and almost uncivilized village, and whatever shocks she had had on the journey from her home in an open gig, to end up with tiny Charlotte, her spectacles on her nose (how she had been teased at school about her short-sightedness!) running out from a house that was situated almost within the graveyard of the looming church, Ellen was far too much of a lady to show them. She graciously descended from the gig, and hugged Charlotte, for they had become dear friends while at school.

'Dearest Ellen, how lovely to see you, and how elegant you look,' Charlotte exclaimed.

'I wish I could say 'How you've grown'

69

— but you haven't,' Ellen laughed mischievously.

'No, I suppose I must resign myself to being a dwarf for ever,' said Charlotte ruefully, for one of the things about herself that irked her most was her lack of height. She pulled at Ellen's hand. 'Come on in and meet my sisters.'

Ellen followed her in, to be greeted by 'a very small, antiquated lady', Aunt Branwell; to be introduced to Emily, who hardly met her eyes before melting into the background again, her reserve taking over. Anne, whom Ellen considered the prettiest of the sisters, shook her hand shyly and said, 'I hope you will have a happy visit.'

'I'm sure I shall,' said Ellen, who had aplomb to meet all difficult social situations, and she smiled so winningly that all the family, even Emily, were charmed.

Papa heard the noises of arrival, and appeared from his study, greeting Ellen with elegant old-world courtesy, and seeing to the comfort of the servant who had accompanied her, and the horse who had pulled the gig. Then Ellen was swept into the kitchen, where Tabby immediately took her under her wing as yet another of her 'childer'.

Ellen accepted everything placidly. Her own luxurious home was certainly very different to the Parsonage, with its scrubbed sandstone floors, windows without curtains, and sparse furniture, and her own family quite a contrast to, say, Mr Brontë, who, she soon found, was rather a recluse, his neck swathed in his white cravat, barely emerging from his study except for his parish duties, and taking all his meals alone there.

She thought Aunt Branwell an amusing relic of other and more racy days. The old lady, in her silk dresses and false front of curls under her huge mob-caps, had never taken to life in the wilds of Yorkshire, and had a horror of catching a chill from the stone floors, so she wore pattens which made a loud clicking sound as she walked.

'She talked a great deal of her younger days,' Ellen recorded later,

> 'the gaieties of her dear native town Penzance in Cornwall; the soft, warm climate, etc. The social life of her younger days she used to recall with regret; she gave one the idea that she had been a belle among her own home acquaintances. She took snuff out of a very pretty gold snuff-box, which she sometimes presented to you with a little laugh, as if she enjoyed the slight shock and astonishment visible in your countenance.'

Aunt Branwell, with her little foibles and eccentricities with which the girls were by now very familiar, did indeed appear odd to a stranger. She was, however, delighted to find a young lady of obvious refinement gracing the Parsonage with her presence, and highly approved of Charlotte's choice of friend. Here was someone to whom she could talk to the social round of which the Brontë girls knew nothing, someone who could *really* understand how she felt, having given up all the gaiety and frivolity of Penzance to come to live in the wilds, but, of course, her duty must come first.

★ ★ ★

Ellen passed a very pleasant visit, accepting everything on the Brontës' terms. She and Charlotte had become close friends while they were at Roe Head together, and Ellen knew in her heart that, though she could out-do the whole family in fashion and elegance and society manners, especially little bespectacled Charlotte, yet Charlotte possessed something she would never have — a wisdom beyond her years, and a wide and deep intellect which had won her prizes at school. Ellen, a simple, sweet-natured girl, tried to learn from her friend, and often asked her advice over what books to read, and so on, during the regular correspondence they had kept up since each had returned home from Roe Head.

She had been curious for a long time about Charlotte's home and family, and now, here they were. She already knew that they lived very quiet lives, for Charlotte had written to tell her about their daily round since she came back from school. She had put:

'*You ask me to give you a description of the manner in which I have passed every day since I left School: this is soon done, as an account of one day is an account of all. In the morning from nine o'clock to half-past twelve, I instruct my Sisters and draw, then we walk till dinner, after dinner I sew till tea time and after tea I either read, write, do a little fancy work or draw, as I please. Thus in one delightful, though somewhat monotonous course my life is passed, I have only been out to tea twice since I came home.*'

Charlotte neglected to mention that beneath the surface of this quiet existence, all the girls and Branwell were living wild and passionate lives in their own secret worlds. She and Branwell had extended the limits of Glasstown to a kingdom they called Angria,

73

and Charlotte was still writing constantly, but now her stories had changed to accounts of extravagant and illicit love, her heroes were cynical men of the world and she was sublimating her own natural sexual desires into her accounts of their affairs. Emily and Anne still lived in Gondal, being drawn deeper and deeper into it every day. Of course, to any outsider, even dear Ellen, all this must be kept a closely hidden secret, and on the surface, they lived the quiet, sedate lives she had described to her friend.

The result was that during Ellen's visit, their guest suspected nothing. She ate the simple, nourishing food that was provided, and rambled with them on the moors, finding that Anne and — surprisingly — Emily too, threw aside their shyness and reserve once they were out amid the beloved bracken and heath.

'Emily can be — well, a bit odd with strangers,' Charlotte had warned her, and Ellen was prepared for unfriendliness from the tall girl with the beautiful liquid eyes, but she soon found that Emily was a different person when out on the moors. She laughed, she was vivacious, and talked as naturally as anyone else. She seemed to blossom, and was like a child — moreover, she would put herself out to do a kindness.

On one occasion, Charlotte was indisposed, and to the amazement of everyone, Emily looked up when hearing that Ellen's proposed walk must be cancelled.

'If Miss Nussey would like a ramble, I'll go with her.'

There was a momentary silence, then, 'Thank you — I'd be delighted,' smiled Ellen, and went to put on her cloak and bonnet.

They set out together, Ellen prepared for a silent and taciturn companion, but as they wandered together, Emily began to talk.

'How do you find our moors, Miss Nussey?'

'They're certainly beautiful,' admitted Ellen, 'but I should think they would be rather desolate in the winter.'

'Yes, the snow can be very deep,' said Emily, 'but they have their own beauty then, too. Beauty's a thing that never changes, not underneath, don't you think? Anything with real worth never alters, in spite of outward appearances.'

Ellen pondered. She threw a swift glance at the tall girl accompanying her, and realized for the first time that Emily was not just an awkward, mawkish member of the family. She had depths of character that she did not reveal at first glance.

As they went on, this impression deepened, and Ellen was fascinated by Emily's strength of mind during their discussion, her intelligence and the genuine kindness underlying her reserve. She found the walk most stimulating.

Charlotte pounced on her as soon as they returned.

'How did Emily behave?'

'We had a wonderful discussion,' said Ellen. 'I like your sister very much, Charlotte.'

'Well!' was all Charlotte could find to say. A moment later, she added, 'She must be coming on. That's the first time she's ever been friendly towards anyone except the family. You've charmed her, Ellen dear, as only you could.' And she hugged her friend.

They took Ellen on other rambles, showing her their favourite spots on the moors, with Branwell accompanying them. There were the ravines, the waterfalls, the sudden banks of primroses, bluebells and moor blossom. When they came to a stream, Branwell, Emily and Anne would sit down and strip off their boots and stockings, and splash through the crystal water like children, but Charlotte and Ellen would not risk such a thing, and waited on the bank until the others had found stones for them to cross by.

They pointed out different mosses, the

prospects and colours in the distance, the birds that fluttered by. The girls took Ellen to one of Emily and Anne's favourite places, which they called the 'Meeting of the Waters', where they could all sit down on slabs of stone amid green turf, broken by several clear springs that came tumbling down the rocky hillside, and Ellen recorded with pleasure that outing where they sat in the clear moorland air, a gentle breeze playing with their hair, and they all laughed and chattered and decided they would call themselves 'The Quartette'.

Emily half-lay on a slab of stone watching the water flow by, and dipped in her hand to play with the tadpoles, making them scurry here and there.

'Look,' she said to the others. 'They're all swimming madly for their lives. I suppose it's the same with them as it is with everything living — the strong survive and the weak go under. Some are brave and some aren't. It's just the same with people. Only the strong, brave ones get on. I despise weakness.'

Ellen could not help noting how much Emily loved the moors and how they seemed her natural habitat, where she lost her reserve and was gay and free. She knew every inch of them, every rock and bush, every expanse of flower and bracken, and she had friends without number in the wild things that lived there. She feared nothing in that limitless, trackless expanse where her mind could open and blossom and she could be herself, free from any restrictions.

Later, Ellen tried to describe Emily.

'Her extreme reserve seemed impenetrable, yet she was intensely lovable; she invited confidence in her moral power. Few people have the gift of looking and smiling as she could look and smile. One of her rare expressive looks was something to remember through life, there was such a depth of soul and feeling, and yet such a shyness of revealing herself.'

The household routine went on undisturbed during Ellen's visit, though the girls, of course, had a holiday from their studies. Meal-times were observed as usual, and every evening, Patrick assembled the family for worship at eight o'clock, and at nine, he locked and barred the Parsonage door, put his head into the parlour to tell the 'children' not to stay up late, and climbed the stairs, pausing on the landing as he did every evening to wind the clock that ticked away there. Ellen even got used to his habit of shooting his pistols — those same pistols that Beth Firth had told Caro about — out through his open window every morning before loading them again, just to make sure they were in good working order.

After their father had gone up to bed, the rest of the family were free to indulge in whatever pleasure they might. While Ellen was with them, they sewed, read or talked, and she watched with interest how inseparable Anne and Emily were, how they always ate, walked, read and sewed together like twins. Anne was still under the supervision of her Aunt, but Emily had now been given leave to organize her own time.

It was not until after Ellen's visit was over, however, that they could settle back to their writing during those precious hours after Papa had gone to bed. Charlotte and Branwell wrote frantically at their Angrian theme, while Emily and Anne were completely wrapped up in the affairs of Gondal.

★ ★ ★

Although she was now old enough, at fifteen, to settle her own day's routine, Emily did not let herself become idle. Like the other girls, she drew and painted, she had her share of household tasks, and later, when the family acquired a piano, she took piano lessons, but most of the time, her mind was far away in Gondal. She listened eagerly to tales her father told them, of some of the extraordinary people he came across in his parish work, and of their doings, and stored up their grimness and their humour for future use. Violence she accepted without a qualm. At the same time as she lived in her dream world, she also realized the truth and bare reality of the world about her, so that she had two sources to draw on when she came to write — the knowledge of reality, and her inner depths of imagination that was forming her own philosophies.

After Charlotte left school, life went on in this manner for some two years. Emily brought home hurt wild things from the moors, and in spite of Aunt's objections, the number of household pets increased. At the time of Ellen's visit, there had been one dog, but later they acquired other dogs, as well as birds, and the following year, Emily and Anne started to write diary-papers one at every interval of four years, and the pets were mentioned. They copied the laconic, terse style which had been used by Byron in his journals, of which the young Brontës had read in the poet's *Life*.

The paper they wrote in the year after Ellen's visit gives a dramatic cameo picture of family life at the Parsonage:

'*November the 24 1834 Monday*
Emily Jane Brontë
Anne Brontë
I fed Rainbow Diamond Snowflake Jasper pheasant (alias) this morning . . . Anne and I have been peeling apples for Charlotte to make us an apple pudding and for Aunt nuts and apples Charlotte said she made puddings perfectly and she was of a quick but limited intellect . . . papa opened the parlour door and gave Branwell a letter saying here Branwell read this and show it to your Aunt and Charlotte — The Gondals are discovering the interior of Gaaldine Sally Mosley is washing in the back kitchen.

'*It is past twelve o'clock Anne and I have not tidied ourselves, done our bed-work or done our lessons and we want to go out to play we are going to have for Dinner Boiled Beef, Turnips, potatoes and apple pudding. The Kitchen is in a very untidy state Anne and I have not done our music exercise which consists of b major Tabby said on my putting a pen in her face Ya pitter pottering there instead of pilling a potate I answered O Dear, O Dear, O dear I will directly . . . '*

At sixteen, Emily's writing and spelling were not what one would expect from the author of a future work of genius, and she speaks with a childishness that belies the deep and mature philosophies she was in the process of working out for herself in her Gondal poetry. But her sense of humour, the racy Yorkshire humour that was to become evident in her later work, is there, as is also the indication that to her, the real world and the world of the imagination are of equal importance. The Gondals exploring Gaaldine are just as vivid to her as Sally Mosley washing in the back kitchen.

★ ★ ★

It was in 1835 that the happy family circle was broken up. It was, of course, inevitable that this would happen eventually, though Emily had never consciously thought about it. She just had some sort of vague hope that everything would carry on as it had for the past two years — studying, doing housework, playing with her pets, romping on the moors, and most of all, drawing deeper and deeper into her dream world,

82

with her family, whom she loved, around her when she needed them.

She had grown more solitary than ever. She was generally recognized by the family as being unsociable, and she avoided visitors to the Parsonage, refused point blank to teach in the Sunday School, and when she had to go shopping in the village, kept her head down and spoke to no one. The reason was because she was afraid of anyone or anything disturbing or penetrating into her inner life, and also, she was becoming more and more aware, as she grew older, that she was in some way different to other people. What mattered to them meant nothing to her, while her own thoughts, poems and ideas, which no-one else must ever be allowed to share, meant everything.

With the family, however, she was as normal as it was possible for her to be. They had had a period of studying music and art, and Emily was a quick learner on the pianoforte, while Branwell, whose talents were many-sided, also played the flute and the organ, and Anne sang. The Parsonage resounded to the music of Bellini, Auber, Meyerbeer and Weber, and especially Handel's oratorios, which Emily and Anne played as duets.

In addition, Patrick had indulged in the

extravagance of painting lessons — largely, it must be admitted, for the benefit of Branwell, who, it was hoped by his doting family, would be admitted to the Royal Academy Schools and would go on to do those 'great things' his boyhood had promised, and bring fame and glory to the name of Brontë.

The girls drew with great enthusiasm, and produced many examples of water-colours, but only Branwell was taught the rudiments of working in oils and portrait-painting, as a preparation for launching himself on the wide sea of life. He was swaggering and full of confidence. Had he not always been the one with the wit, the charm of the family, the great hope of his sisters and father? He could do anything he turned his hand to — write, paint, play an instrument, tell a tale — and as well as that, he was not like the girls, living sheltered lives within the walls of the Parsonage. Branwell had gone out to find other companions, and was a great favourite with the patrons and customers at the Black Bull, his easy, charming personality helping him to get along with everyone.

The question was, what would he eventually become? Poet, artist, or what? Patrick seriously considered his son to be greatly gifted as an artist, and now that Branwell was nearly eighteen, it was time to take action and send him to the Academy Schools. This meant that all the money Patrick could afford — as well as what he could beg or borrow from friends — would be lavished on his son's future, should he be accepted as a pupil, and there would be nothing over for the girls, but they took this as only natural. Branwell had always been the brilliant one, and after all, he was a boy. They could not expect Papa to spend money on them if Branwell needed it.

At this most opportune moment, an invitation came out of the blue. Miss Wooler, Charlotte's former headmistress at Roe Head, wrote to ask whether Charlotte would like to return to the school, but not as a pupil. A post was now available as an assistant teacher, and part of her salary would be free schooling for another of her sisters.

This was what Charlotte had hoped for, and yet dreaded. The chance to earn her own living — but at the expense of leaving home and being parted yet again from Angria and the latest hero of her tales, the Duke of Zamorna, rich, passionate, amoral and thoroughly irresistible. Aunt had taught her lessons well. Duty must come first, and Charlotte not only accepted the post, but even planned to put aside part of her salary in order to help out with expenses for Branwell, which Papa could not afford. Besides, she knew and liked Miss Wooler, so it might not be as bad as all that — it was not, after all, as though she was going as governess to a strange family.

And there was no question about which sister should benefit from the free schooling. Emily of course, the next in age, should come, and then she too, like Charlotte, would be qualified and in a position to become a teacher and earn a living for herself. Later, perhaps, the same course could be followed with Anne, thought Patrick, as he wrote to Beth Firth and her husband, who lived not too far from Roe Head, asking them to be so kind as to keep a watchful eye on his girls and keep them from 'the ways of this delusive and ensnaring world'.

To Patrick, it all seemed ideal. Unfortunately, the shock to Emily when she learned that she was to be sent away to school — parted from her home and her beloved moors, her pets and all the surroundings so necessary to her dream-world — was like a blow to the heart.

'I won't go,' she said flatly to Charlotte. 'Anne can go in my place.'

'But Papa has settled everything now, and in any case, it is your turn, Emily. Don't you want to have a chance in life? Don't you want an education?' demanded Charlotte.

'I want to stay here. I don't want to go away,' said Emily.

'But how can you know whether you'll be happy until you've tried it?' Charlotte said coaxingly. 'The school is very good, Emily, and the Misses Wooler are lovely people. I didn't want to go at first, but I was happy there, and I made friends.'

'I don't want friends. I don't need them,' said Emily, stoney-faced.

Charlotte was silent, looking at the stormy, tormented eyes of her loved, but elusive sister. Then she spoke.

'I know how you feel, dear, but at least we'll be together, and it won't be for long. Things can't always stay the same, you know. We're all growing up, and you'll be much better off for an education. Can't you try, just this once?'

Emily gave a deep sigh, and spread her hands. For Charlotte's sake, she gave in.

'All right, then. I'll go.'

'You won't be sorry, Emily,' Charlotte assured her, and pressed her hand.

'No, I'm sure I won't,' said Emily, and turned away, whistling the dogs to accompany her for one of the last rambles she would be able to have for some time on her deeply loved moors. She felt as though her soul was breaking, being torn out of her breast. How could she leave them, the rocks and heath and wild things, the streams and brooks and dells, every one of which she knew by heart? Yet her common-sense recognized that what Charlotte had said was true, and at least she would be with her sister. She tried to bow her head and take her fate calmly, and almost succeeded in persuading herself that all would be well.

She packed her things for school in a silence even more deep than usual, made her preparations, and on the day before her seventeenth birthday, she and Charlotte set off to Roe Head.

5

Patrick's fond hope of seeing his family happily settled, Branwell at the Academy Schools and Charlotte and Emily at Roe Head, were soon to be dashed. Branwell was the first to let his doting father down. He set off jauntily enough for London, the great metropolis he had dreamed of so often, with letters of introduction and samples of his work to show the masters he hoped would be his future teachers; but little did Patrick realize that this seeming genius, this boy who at nineteen had never before left home, and who had always been regarded as the darling of the family who would do great things, was emotionally unable to cope with reality when any effort was demanded from him.

Like Emily, he had spent so long in a secret world that when it came to facing the real thing, self-doubts, fright and the inherent instability of his character, which was mercurial, but basically without the foundation rooted in real life that he needed, all combined to send him scuttling for the nearest refuge, which in his case was drink — with which he was already familiar — and drugs in the form of laudanum, which could be purchased easily in those days.

He could not face it! That was the simple truth. He could not possibly go and compete with other men, better men than himself, possibly, for a place in the Academy Schools, for inwardly, the great hero of Angria, cut off from his secret life, was trembling and fearful, a small boy who wanted nothing more than to escape back to the safety of home where he was petted and indulged, and once more master of all he surveyed.

So he went, as arranged, to his lodgings at the Chapter Coffee House, Paternoster Row, lost and frightened in the bustle of the great city, feeling himself to be nothing compared to the hurry and scurry everywhere, and he spent his time lying dismally on the sofa, knowing in every fibre of his being that he did not belong. He made no attempt to present himself at the Academy Schools. He found his escape, and some small degree of consolation, at the Castle Tavern in Holborn, spending the money his father had so painstakingly saved for him on rum, until, after seven days of wandering about London like a lost soul, he had spent all his money, and there was nothing for it but to take a coach on the first stage of his journey back to

Haworth and home, a lost, pitiful, degraded and beaten man.

His shame at what had happened, and the way in which he had collapsed morally at trying to face reality, was such that he could not possibly admit to Papa and Aunt what had happened, so he invented a story that he had been robbed on the coach to London, and told them that in any case, he had decided that his real career lay in literature not art.

Papa and Aunt were baffled and bitterly disappointed, but not more so than Branwell himself. He had been tried and had been found wanting, and he knew even then that he did not have it in him to confront the real world on its own terms, so he turned back to his means of escape almost frantically, continuing to write of Angria, drinking heavily and beginning to experiment with laudanum, that fascinating drug that induced a feeling of power and omnipotence. Branwell was no fighter. When too much was demanded from him, he simply gave up the struggle before it began, and ran to hide. This was to be the sad and pitiful story of his life.

Meanwhile, Charlotte and Emily had settled in at Roe Head, where Charlotte soon found that it was very different being a teacher than it was to being a pupil. She was proud, but she must remember now that she was an employee, and it was her duty to slave at teaching, which she hated — for it did not come easily to her, especially when dealing with young or dull girls — for a mere pittance. Moreover, she saw little of Emily during the day, and it was only when they retired together to the bed they shared that they could exchange confidences and try to comfort each other.

For Emily, from the first day she entered the school, every moment was utter torture. She had never been away from home in ten years, and knew nothing of life other than the free-and-easy existence she had enjoyed both mentally and physically at the Parsonage, but at school — however pleasant a school it was — she was physically confined, like a prisoner, her day governed by rules and lesson-times.

Mentally, her mind too was confined. She was not allowed to study as she pleased, delving deep into any subject that interested her, as she had done at home, and the superficiality of the lessons both bored her and filled her with scorn. Committing dates to memory, and the lady-like recital of facts that followed in lesson after lesson brought her mind to the verge of breakdown. She hated the time-tables, she hated the lessons, and most of all, she hated the importance that was put on learning manners and social graces. Emily felt no need or desire for social graces, and what was even worse was that Beth Firth, now Mrs Franks, carried out Mr Brontë's request and took a friendly interest in the girls' progress, which Emily saw as interference in their affairs.

She was like a wild bird of the moors, caged and beating frantically against its bars. She was imprisoned and helpless, and a terrible sense of frustration filled her that mounted and mounted until it was almost unbearable. She had no one to talk to — except, occasionally, Charlotte — she was parted from Anne, who had shared her life for so long, and the most dreadful thing of all was that she had no opportunity to escape into the dream-world of Gondal.

But Emily was no weakling like Branwell. For Charlotte's sake, and the sake of the family, she tried to fight against her crippling homesickness, but the effort almost tore her apart. She could not eat, she could not sleep, and under the misery of the strain of each passing day, she became pale and thin, a ghost of her former self. Even her escape, when it came, did not come from her own efforts, but from those of Charlotte, who remembered all too clearly the deaths of Maria and Elizabeth, and who was seized with a terrible fear that Emily might die too, if nothing was done. Miss Wooler would never understand, but Papa and Aunt knew of Emily's devotion to her home, and Charlotte wrote to them, urgently asking that they recall Emily from school. They did as she asked, and a pale and sickly Emily was sent home, where, reunited with her beloved moors and the routine that she knew and loved, and most of all, her own world of Gondal, she soon regained her health and strength.

Charlotte later tried to explain exactly why Emily had not been able to settle down away from her home, though in congenial surroundings:

> 'My sister Emily loved the moors,' she wrote. 'Flowers brighter than the rose bloomed in the blackest of the heath for her; out of a sullen hollow in a livid hillside her mind could make an Eden. She found in the bleak solitude many and dear delights; and not the least and best loved — was liberty.
>
> 'Liberty was the breath of Emily's nostrils; without it, she perished. The change from her own home to a school,

*and from her own very noiseless very
secluded, but unrestricted and inartificial
mode of life, to one of disciplined routine
(though under the kindliest auspices) was
what she failed in enduring. Her nature
proved here too strong for her fortitude.
Every morning when she wrote, the vision
of home and the moors rushed on her, and
darkened and saddened the day that lay
before her. Nobody knew what ailed her
but me — I knew only too well . . . '*

Inwardly, Charlotte knew that it was not
only the moors but Gondal that Emily
missed most of all. She herself pined bitterly
for Angria, but she realized that though
she could — albeit with a terrible effort
— conquer her longing, Emily had given
herself completely to her secret world and
could not exist without it. It seemed to be
one of the facts that would have to be
accepted, but Emily could not settle down
happily now away from home.

Anne, docile and pious, came to Roe
Head in her place, but Charlotte found her
fifteen-year-old sister no substitute for the
wild, untamable Emily, and almost resented
the fact that she had to spend some of
her precious earnings on Anne's clothes
and small wants. Charlotte gradually sank

into an unexplained neurasthenia, which she aggravated by allowing herself to live a double life — one as Miss Brontë of Roe Head, the other in Angria, into which she could only escape at very infrequent moments, for her day was taken up with duties and chores. She, too, like Emily, was a fighter. She battled on, sinking deeper in misery and depression, but determined to keep going, for what else could she do?

Back at the Parsonage, Emily was faced with the prospect of Branwell, who, like herself, had failed in his first battle with the world, and all her sympathy and protective instincts were aroused by the pitiful figure he now cut. To see her brilliant, confident brother creeping round the village, uncertain of himself, was something that wrung her heart, and she generously gave him the unstinting belief that she thought his failure had been because he had refused to conform, and that he would, as time went on, still show that he was superior to other people.

They had never been particularly close before, but now, as Papa and Aunt left them alone together more and more often, they began to grow closer, and in spite of herself, Emily found a good deal, both real and imaginary, in Branwell's character to study and to give her food for thought. He had become in her eyes a solitary hero doing battle against the established order of things, and she was certain he would eventually overcome all and heroically redeem himself.

★ ★ ★

For two years, Emily continued her quiet life at home while Charlotte and Anne were still at Roe Head, and Branwell was making sporadic efforts to get into print, and scribbing furiously at Angria, exchanging news of his 'infernal world' in letters to Charlotte, who, while still struggling to teach, lived whenever she could in that glorious and glamorous world also, but the bright visions she glimpsed whilst living her double life sent her first deeper into depression and then into desperate religious melancholy. Were her day-dreamings of illicit and passionate love and her hallucinations of her heroes standing before her in all their glory, sinful? Was Angria itself and its creation sinful? Was she a wicked, lost soul? She wrote letters to Ellen, where, though she could not tell her friend the real reason for her despair, she tried to explain her feelings.

'If you knew my thoughts; the dreams that absorb me; and the fiery imagination

that at times eats me up and makes me feel Society as it is, wretchedly insipid, you would pity and I dare say despise me . . .'

Ellen wrote back eagerly, trying to comfort her friend and exhorting her to be pure and to pray for guidance, but her letters only drove home to Charlotte that she *could* not give up her secret life and the erotic, imaginative world that she and Branwell had created between them. Charlotte struggled on, tormented and suffering, but refusing to give in.

Emily had no such qualms about Gondal. She lost herself in it completely during the time she was at home, though she still managed to keep up with her studies, and matured in a way that she could never have done if she had still been at school. She pondered on themes of guilt and failure, and the ever-present mystery of inherent evil. She practised her music and read widely; she taught herself German, and tried to perfect her French; she talked to Tabby often, extracting Yorkshire tales of fairies and the exploits of local people immortalized in folk-lore; she studied Branwell, his mind, his passions, and what drove him. Already a 'hero' figure was beginning to form in her mind — an 'anti-hero', in fact, a 'dark man' who scorned the world and who would later become Heathcliff.

★ ★ ★

December 1836, and Charlotte and Anne were home for Christmas. Once more Branwell and his eldest sister could dream of Angria as much as they liked.

'I've been thinking,' Branwell said to Charlotte. 'I mean to try my luck as a professional writer. That way, your time's your own, you can write when and where you want to, it's the perfect solution to everything.'

'If only I could become a professional writer,' Charlotte said slowly, her voice full of longing. 'I'd escape from all the drudgery of teaching for ever.'

'What I've thought of doing is writing to somebody famous — Wordsworth, possibly, and sending some of my work,' Branwell went on, ruffling his mass of hair until it stood on end.

'I wonder if Robert Southey would answer if I wrote to him?' said Charlotte, involuntarily. 'Oh, let's do it, Brany.'

So two hopeful communications were sent off — but alas, both were doomed to failure.

Wordsworth, to whom Branwell wrote, was so disgusted by the tactlessness and tone of the letter that he did not bother to reply. Southey, from whom Charlotte sought advice, wrote back that writing never had been, and never should be, a woman's task, and more or less told her to stop day-dreaming and get on with her ordinary life. Needless to say, both Branwell and Charlotte were deeply disappointed by the results of their enquiries.

To add to the gloom, Tabby fell in the village street and broke her leg, necessitating the family having to nurse her at the Parsonage, and so a visit from Ellen had to be cancelled. Most of the burden of nursing and looking after the rest of the family fell on Emily, for Aunt spent most of her time in her room, and did not undertake rough work, but Emily shouldered the work cheerfully. She became the family housekeeper, baking the bread, which was never less than excellent, and taking on the large weekly family wash. The competent and practical side of her nature fitted her well for this role, and both then and later, she proved to be a wonderful housekeeper.

While she kneaded the bread, her German grammar was propped up beside her, and while she washed and scrubbed, her mind was busy with ideas which she jotted down later on bits of paper. She, at least, was happy with her lot, even if the others were not, though her imagination was not satisfied with life, as it appeared to her, and she pondered, withdrawing deeper and deeper into her own spirit, looking for answers to metaphysical problems.

Night-time was the magic time for Emily. She would lie on her narrow bed and gaze out through the uncurtained window, while visions formed in her mind, inspired by the awesomeness of moon, night and stars. She was a poet of darkness; and darkness and the realms of night were fast becoming her domain.

'There shines the moon, at noon of
    night — ,' she wrote.
'Vision of glory — Dream of light!
'Holy as heaven — undimmed and
    pure,
'Looking down on the lonely moor — .'

The next year, there was an upheaval in Emily's life. One of the outside influences was the coming to the throne of the young Queen Victoria, who had always been an inspiration, and Emily wove the theme of coronations into her Gondal plot. Charlotte and Anne returned after the summer holidays to their school, which had been moved from Roe Head to Dewsbury Moor, which was not such a healthy place — and Emily suddenly left home and took a position as a teacher at Law Hill, a school with some forty pupils not far from Halifax.

It was a sudden decision. Emily saw an advertisement, and answered it. She was feeling guilty, knowing how Charlotte and Anne felt about leaving the family home, and seeing how bravely they were enduring their exile at Miss Wooler's school. Papa was worrying, as always, about money — perhaps she could do a little to ease his burden, now that Tabby was back in command of the kitchen. And in addition, Branwell had had another stab at facing the world and had gone as an usher to a boys' school in the same region as Law Hill, and Emily thought it might comfort him to have her near.

She was nineteen now, and realized just as much as Charlotte and Anne did that they must all help to earn their keep. She determined that this time, she would stick it out away from home, though no sooner had she made the decision to go, and left for Law Hill than she felt in her heart that she had done the wrong thing — wrong for her. She had failed once in her efforts to conquer reality, but she was older now, and owed it to the rest of the family to make at least one more attempt.

Her new home stood high up on Southowram Bank, overlooking Halifax, and at least she could see hills around her, but her heart was heavy as she arrived to take up her duties. The school was large, and she had no experience as a teacher, and this time, reality proved even worse than her schooldays at Roe Head. She wrote to Charlotte, who commented anxiously in a note to Ellen:

'I have had one letter from her since her departure . . . it gives an appalling account of her duties — hard labour from six in the morning until near eleven at night, with only one half-hour of exercise between. This is slavery. I fear she will never stand it.'

In her misery, Emily was, perhaps, overstating her case, but this was how her duties appeared to her, and Charlotte's dire prediction soon came true. Emily was, for one thing, completely unsuited to be a teacher. One day, for instance, she lost her temper with her class of lively girls, and shouted at them,

'You're all the same! The only admirable

103

individual in this whole establishment is the dog!'

'Hardly the way to treat the daughters of gentlefolk, who are paying for their education, my dear,' said Miss Patchett, the headmistress, sharply when she heard about it.

'It's true,' said Emily, through her teeth.

'If you cannot keep your temper better than that, I fear we will have to reconsider your suitability for the post, but I am sure you will settle down,' smiled Miss Patchett, with the venom, Emily thought, of a snake. She left the head teacher's room feeling that her employer was nothing but a tyrant.

The moments when she could sit alone and write were few. The poetry she produced at Law Hill all speaks of her longing for her home, and after six months of struggle, she gave in her notice and thankfully departed, the journey back to Haworth seeming to her like the road leading from Hell to Heaven.

Branwell meantime had long since left his position at the boys' school, where his rather short stature and characteristics such as a quiff of carroty hair and distinctive features made him a figure of fun amongst the boys; and Anne had also returned home in the Christmas of 1837.

Anne had shared a bed with her Aunt

during her formative years, and was so mild and docile in her behaviour that amongst the rebellious sisters, her quietness and meek manners often made her overlooked. Her Aunt's influence was strongest in this youngest of all the children, and Anne suffered a great deal under the constant prompting of Aunt Branwell on religious topics, feeling that she was not, and never could be, as good as God wanted her to be. She was afraid she would be eternally damned, but, being Anne, she kept her fears to herself, and suffered in silence. She never spoke about religion, although Mary Taylor, another of Charlotte's friends, brought up the subject once when she was staying at the Parsonage, and declared that her religion was between God and herself.

Emily, who was lying on the hearthrug, simply said, 'That's right,' and in those two words, all she ever uttered on the subject of her beliefs, she expressed her whole philosophy.

★ ★ ★

Anne had dutifully gone to Roe Head in Emily's place, but she too missed her home and Gondal. She never complained, however, and it took two years for the combination of homesickness, longing for her dreams and her writing, and fears for her soul, to break her health and spirits. She too came to the verge of a breakdown — though not so dramatic as Emily's had been. It began with a neglected cold, and her low spirits led her into a state of mental depression and physical illness. She received spiritual consolation from the Reverend James la Trobe, who was called in to visit her, and his creed, kindlier and more merciful than Aunt Branwell's, comforted her distraught heart, but her illness persisted.

Charlotte, again remembering Maria and Elizabeth, saw her sister panting, coughing and shaking with fever, and believed she had consumption. She went straight to Miss Wooler, and demanded that Anne should be sent home, as she was dying. Miss Wooler was kind, but firmly put the matter on one side, and after a few more agonizing days of watching Anne's suffering, Charlotte stormed into Miss Wooler's room.

'You're indifferent and hard-hearted,' she said, her voice quivering with passion.

Tears sprang to Miss Wooler's eyes under the onslaught of her usually docile Miss Brontë, as they faced each other across her desk.

'I shall write to your father,' she said

tremulously, 'and tell him what you have said to me.'

And so she did, but Patrick read between the lines, knew that something must be wrong, and sent for both his daughters immediately.

'I'll never set foot in this place again,' vowed Charlotte, angrily packing her things together, but at this point, Miss Wooler sent for her and apologized.

'I — I didn't realize Anne was so ill — and — well, Charlotte, I am very fond of you and I would be sorry to lose you. Please say that you will come back.'

The one thing that could always melt Charlotte's heart was for anyone to say they were fond of her and that she meant a lot to them, and despite herself, she found herself promising to return once she had seen Anne safely home. So she took her sister back to the Parsonage and saw her settled in, pale and thin, but on the road to recovery, and forced herself back to her grim tasks and her double life at Miss Wooler's, but as the months slipped by, her misery and depression and mental torment grew — being made all the worse by the fact that she knew both Emily and Anne had escaped and were together under the Parsonage roof — until her life became unbearable, a waking nightmare.

Inevitably, she too fell ill, and when the doctor who was called to her asked gently what the trouble was, she could keep it to herself no longer. Overwork, tension and strain, terrible anxiety, were all swept aside as she whispered only, 'If I could just — go home — .'

'You shall — indeed, you must,' he assured her, and told Miss Wooler that if Charlotte valued her life and sanity, she must return home as Anne had done. So in the balmy air of May, she came back to Haworth, having left Miss Wooler's for good, and like Emily, she began to recover her health and spirits in the familiar atmosphere of the beloved home. After all their battles and all their efforts to come to terms with life, all the family had, for the moment, a brief respite from their labours, and life went on happily at the Parsonage as though they had never left it — though each of them was scarred by the experiences they had gone through.

★ ★ ★

Branwell was the first to leave the family fold again. Full of confidence once more, he

108

persuaded Patrick to set him up in Bradford as a portrait painter, and Aunt paid the fees for him to have more painting lessons, but the lack of staying power that had failed him before, and his natural ability to get into debt and neglect his duties meant that within a few months he was back home — once more a failure.

This was the year that Patrick was enabled, through a grant from the Curates' Aid Society, to keep a curate; and also the year that Charlotte received two proposals of marriage. The first was from Henry Nussey, Ellen's brother. Fortunately, Charlotte did not love the Reverend Nussey, and secretly longed for a masterful, passionate wooer like her Angrian heroes, so she refused him. Little did she know that he had cold-bloodedly drawn up a list of young ladies who might make him suitable wives and helpmates — and she was not even the first on the list — so she had a lucky escape from what would probably have been a loveless and unhappy marriage.

Within five months, however, she had a second proposal, even more ludicrous than the first.

'Prepare for a hearty laugh!' she wrote to Ellen. 'The other day Mr Hodgson, Papa's

109

*former curate now a vicar . . . came over
to spend the day with us, bringing with
him his curate . . . Mr Bryce . . . a young
Irish clergyman from Dublin University.
It was the first time we had any of us
seen him but however, after the manner
of his countrymen, he soon made himself
at home . . . '*

Charlotte was her natural self when
surrounded by her family at the Parsonage,
free from the shyness that haunted her so
often elsewhere, and after only an afternoon
and evening in her company, the fervent Mr
Bryce sent her, a few days later, an ardent
proposal.

*'Well!' she wrote in her letter to Ellen. 'I
have heard of love at first sight, but this
beats all.'*

Naturally, her answer had to be a refusal,
and she added regretfully to her friend that
she was obviously cut out to be an old maid,
and had in fact been resigned to that prospect
since she was twelve.

Still, at least she had been proposed to
— twice — and that helped a little to
lighten the fact that she and Anne, who
had now fully recovered from her illness,

had of necessity to try and find positions as governesses with private families. They could not remain at home, earning nothing. They must help out with the family budget, while Emily was to take over the housekeeping, for Tabby was growing old and infirm.

In all, Charlotte and Anne each held two positions as governesses at various times, and the experiences, though often unpleasant, were to provide valuable material for their novels. They made a start in 1839, when Anne found a position with Mrs Ingham of Blake Hall, Mirfield, in April, and the following month Charlotte went off to a Mrs Sidgwick of Stonegappe, near Skipton. They did not remain in these first positions for very long, and Charlotte later went to a Mrs White, with whom she stayed for less than nine months. Anne found a happier position later when she was employed at Thorp Green. She remained there for several years, a valued assistant to the family.

While the other girls were coming and going, Emily stayed at home, running the house, until the year 1842, when she was twenty-three. She worked on her Gondal world, her thoughts probing deeper and deeper, taking new turns, wandering down mystical byways as she wrote her poetry. She was teaching herself to be a writer of genius, but all that she did was secret, and no one was allowed to penetrate into the dark recesses of her soul, where the pattern that was to be *Wuthering Heights* was beginning to form.

6

'But who can have sent them?'

'Oh, listen, mine reads 'Fair Ellen, Fair Ellen — '.'

'No listen to mine. 'Away fond love — '.'

The girls and Ellen were all chattering away like magpies. Only Emily stood aloof, watching with an indulgent smile. It was 14th February, 1840, Ellen was paying them a visit at the Parsonage, and the most amazing thing had happened. The post had brought every one of them a Valentine — the first they had ever received in their lives!

'It must be Miss Celia Amelia up to her tricks,' laughed Charlotte, fingering the precious paper.

'It couldn't be anyone else,' added Anne, softly.

Emily said nothing, but her eyes were glowing as she looked on at her sisters' pleasure.

'The postmark is Bradford, though,' exclaimed Ellen.

'Do you suppose he could have gone all that way to post them?' demanded

Charlotte, peering short-sightedly through her spectacles.

'It would be like him to try and please us,' said Anne.

The subject of their conversation entered the room just then. He was Mr Brontë's latest curate, the Reverend William Weightman, who had been enlivening their existence for some time now. He was a classical graduate from Durham, but even more interesting to the girls, he was young, handsome, and very flirtatious, with a silver tongue that could frame a compliment to turn anyone's head, and a way with him that could thaw the hardest heart. Even Aunt suffered his nonsense with a smile, and Emily watched him indulgently as he collected a whole range of feminine hearts throughout the district. Perhaps to defend their own hearts against his charm, they had christened him 'Miss Celia Amelia' and referred to him as 'her'.

But it was too late in one case. Anne had already begun to love him. He was a man one could admire and respect, for beneath the outward frivolity, he was intelligent, well-read and a gentleman by nature. However, she knew that he had a fiancée back home in Westmorland, and she never revealed her feelings as they deepened towards him.

On his entry into the parlour, the girls

clustered round him.

'I protest, I protest, I know nothing about them at all,' he cried, when they accused him of sending the Valentines. 'You must all have secret admirers.'

'What a dangerous character you are,' commented Emily, who rarely spoke, from her place in the corner. 'I think you need watching — especially as far as Miss Nussey is concerned. I'll constitute myself her personal bodyguard from now on.'

And during their walks on the moors, when Mr Weightman tried to lure Ellen away from the others in order to flirt with her, Emily always followed in their wake.

'Really, you are a regular Major,' exclaimed Mr Weightman, and always referred to her after that as 'The Major', a nickname which gave her sense of the ridiculous something to chuckle at.

'It suits you, too, Emily,' said Charlotte, laughing, as she looked at the tall figure of her sister marching along with her dog at her side and whistling.

But Emily did not reply. She was guarding her sisters as well as Ellen from losing their hearts to the frivolous clergyman. She knew that she herself was in no danger, but she was well aware of the possible follies of the others. At any rate, all of them except Anne escaped heart-free, and Anne kept her love to herself, to write about when she was alone, and dream over in her quiet moments.

Later, Willy Weightman admitted that he had indeed sent the Valentines, and had walked the eight miles to Bradford to post them, so that the girls would not guess his secret. It was a typical gesture of his generous heart. He made other plans for them, too. When he was asked to give a lecture on the classics at the Mechanics Institute in Keighley, he thought the girls would like to be there, and an invitation was cordially sent from Mr Drury, the rector of Keighley, who asked them to tea first, and reassured them that they would be escorted to and from the lecture — for of course, they would have to walk there and back, four miles each way. Patrick and Aunt were doubtful, but at last, permission was given, and in great excitement, the girls set out on this unexpected treat, duly escorted by Mr Weightman.

They thoroughly enjoyed themselves, and were accompanied home by Mr Weightman and Mr Drury, arriving at midnight, where Aunt was waiting with hot coffee — enough for the girls, but not for their escorts.

'Oh, how cross Aunt was,' laughed Charlotte afterwards, recalling Aunt's discomfiture over the little social contretemps, but it had been worth it, and the sisters grew fonder of Mr Weightman than ever, for although he had faults, he had compassion and generosity of heart too.

Emily, busy in her dream-world, remained unaffected by the pangs of love, and Charlotte took refuge in lofty cynicism, but Anne quietly nurtured her affection, though he never knew about it, and she never showed it. Charlotte wrote to Ellen:

'He sits opposite to Anne at Church sighing softly and looking out of the corners of his eyes to attract her attention; and Anne is so quiet, her look so downcast, they are a picture.'

Round about this time, while Charlotte and Anne were at home between their governessing posts, Branwell set out again to try and conquer the world, this time as a booking clerk at Sowerby Bridge railway station. Railways then were similar to the nuclear age of today, something new and exciting. At the end of a six-month trial period, he found his employers were satisfied with his work — a novel experience for him — and was promoted to 'Clerk in Charge' at the smaller station of Luddenden Foot, but there was time on his hands, and he was left to his own devices. He became bored with the work, and spent most of his time scribbling verses and sketching — and drinking at an all too convenient public house. He was also still experimenting with laudanum, and the result was only too predictable.

Branwell was ignominiously dismissed for carelessness and neglect of duty, and returned home more dispirited than ever, just as the girls were on the point of undertaking the most ambitious and hopeful scheme they had ever tried, and the Parsonage was buzzing with excitement.

★ ★ ★

But before this scheme was launched, Emily had developed far with her poetry and her thinking. The great influences on her life had been nature, the moors, her father's encouragement of independent thought, and the tales that he and Tabby told — one full of Celtic imagery and passion, the other permeated with Yorkshire grimness and humour. In addition, Emily, as had the other girls, had been affected a good deal by the Byronic hero-image. She had written of outlaws, prisoners, bandits and exiles in her Gondal saga, all derived from her reading of

118

Byron, and her heroes and heroines defied both man and God in furious desperation. From Byron came the idea of a Satanic being who is nevertheless always conscious of his own greatness, but who has fallen by the sin of pride. The power of the mind, the ability to shape one's own destiny, all these ideas came from her Byronic reading.

In addition, as she lay in her narrow bed, looking at the moon and stars, bits and pieces of information and isolated incidents floated through her mind, all of which were to fall into place in the mosaic which was to be *Wuthering Heights*.

When she recalled Byron overhearing a girl he believed loved him saying scornfully, 'Do you think I could care for that lame boy?' it was a foreshadowing of Catherine's passionate outburst, 'It would degrade me to marry Heathcliff', and Heathcliff's mad and furious dash from the house to disappear into the bustling world for three long years, and return embittered and determined on revenge, not against Catherine but against the world which had made him what he was.

There were other echoes from the works of Byron, but Emily did not lift them consciously from his writing. Her story was mapped out in her mind — it so happened that sometimes her thoughts and Byron's coincided. Milton too influenced her. The fall of Satan — this idea of inherent evil which she had pondered on for so long — the fact that the supposedly evil man had acted only according to the nature God had given him, made her sympathize and pity the fallen one's desire for his lost rights, and for vengeance.

While all this was forming in her mind, the side of her that loved nature was following in the tradition of Sir Walter Scott and ballad poetry, which she loved. They taught her the ballad form she used so often in her poetry, and immediacy of attack, vigour and drama, terse and vital dialogue. The haunting quality of ballad poetry was another influence that was to spread its wings over *Wuthering Heights*.

Emily wrote two kinds of poetry. The first were ordinary poems on such subjects as her love for the moors and her home. She and Charlotte expressed the same feelings, Emily when she wrote:

'*There is a spot mid barren hills*
    Where winter howls and driving rain,
But if the dreary tempest chills
    There is a light that warms again.

'The house is old, the trees are bare
    And moonless bends the misty dome
But what on earth is half so dear,
    So longed for as the hearth of home?'

and Charlotte when she confided to Henry Nussey, while she was pondering on the life of an 'exile' as a governess:

'My home is humble and unattractive to strangers, but to me it contains what I shall find nowhere else in the world — the profound, the intense affection which brothers and sisters feel for each other when their minds are cast in the same mould, their ideas drawn from the same source — when they have clung to each other from childhood and when disputes have never sprung up to divide them.'

But Emily also wrote what she called her 'Gondal poems', which were part of her Gondal saga, and contained drama and incident relevant to the Gondal story. Many people have thought — indeed, taken it for granted — that all Emily's poems were autobiographical, but they were not. Intense emotions found in such poems as:

'Cold in the earth — and the deep snow piled above thee
  Far, far removed, cold in the dreary grave!
Have I forgot, my only Love, to love thee,
  Sever'd at last by Time's all severing wave?'

have been assumed to have been felt by Emily. Surely the woman who wrote that must have had a love affair? Must have suffered the agony of grief on losing her lover? Emily never had a love affair with anyone, and the emotion is felt by her Gondal character who speaks the poem. The genius lies in the way she could transmute the emotions of her characters into convincing reality, for to her, Gondal was reality itself.

Again, people have wondered how an inexperienced girl, leading a sheltered existence where she seldom left home and met few people, could obtain such a wide and mature outlook on life. The truth was that Emily was an observer. Every little incident that happened in the family, every place she visited, every tale or story she heard, were stored up and used in her work. She watched the love affairs of others, but never loved

122

herself; she watched the behaviour patterns of her brother and sisters, and wove them into her narrative when she came to write *Wuthering Heights.* And the result was more convincing than if she had lived a lifetime of passionate incident and emotion herself.

Tabby became immortalized as Nelly, the narrator of the tale; Branwell served as a model for both Mr Lockwood and, in part, Heathcliff; the farmhouse of Top Withens, up on the moors, gave her the situation for the farmhouse in her tale, while its façade was taken from the ornate façade of High Sunderland Hall, with which she became familiar when working at Law Hill. Ponden House, where Mr Brontë's church trustee lived, inspired the dignity of Thrushcross Grange, even down to the description of the room where Emily placed Catherine's death-bed scene, and there were other little details that wove their way into her story. Amongst the staff at Law Hill, for instance, was a lady whose name was Earnshaw, and the outline of the tale that was to give her the basic plot of *Wuthering Heights* belonged to the history of a family she came to hear about, again whilst living at Law Hill.

Of course, she did not know at the time what her subconscious was doing with all these details, but was still occupied with her poetry when she returned from Law Hill. Now, however, her verse deepened and took a different turn. She was happy enough at home, doing the housework and looking after the family, but a spiritual element was becoming more marked in her work. She rebelled in spirit against life itself, and looked round her for a means of escape, spiritual escape, from the confines of day to day existence:

> '*I'm happiest when most away*
> *I can bear my soul from its home of*
> *clay*
> *On a windy night when the moon is*
> *bright*
> *And the eye can wander through worlds*
> *of light —*

> '*When I am not and none beside —*
> *Nor earth nor sea nor cloudless sky —*
> *But only spirit wandering wide*
> *Through infinite immensity.*'

As she grew towards womanhood, in circumstances which were, to say the least, unusual — for she guarded the privacy of her little bedroom where she dreamed her dreams, and led an almost hermit-like existence wandering the moors alone — her

124

mind wandered even further afield into the realms of the metaphysical. She often struggled to express what she wanted to say in her poems, and could not do so, much to her self-disgust and frustration. It was now that a new element entered her poetry.

Emily never loved, nor had a love affair, but much of her later work is written as though to an actual physical person or presence. It was as though she surrendered herself to an outside force, which visited her and became the most important thing in her life. Here, she describes 'its coming':

'I'll come when thou art saddest
Laid alone in the darkened room;
When the mad day's mirth has vanished,
And the smile of joy is banished
From evening's chilly gloom . . .

'Listen, 'tis just the hour,
The awful time for thee;
Dost thou not feel upon thy soul
A flood of strange sensations roll,
Forerunners of a sterner power,
Heralds of me?'

The only way to describe this mystical visitor is to say that her great desire for freedom took on actual shape and form, and occasionally, her longing to be let loose from the bounds of a physical existence and to be one with nature itself — the life of the universe — brought her visions that were ecstatic — but which, alas, faded all too soon as her earthly body reached out to claim her again.

These experiences took the place of the earthly love she never knew, and the ecstasy felt during them can be compared to the ecstasy of sexual intimacy. She longed for her visitations, she could not live without them, for without them she was only half a person and the thing she cherished most was missing from her life, leaving it barren and cheerless. When the vision faded, the aftermath was terrible:

'*Oh, dreadful is the check, — intense the agony,*
When the ear begins to hear and the eye begins to see;
When the pulse begins to throb, the brain to think again,
The soul to feel the flesh and the flesh to feel the chain!'

It was impossible for her to record these visions and experiences without using the language of love, for nothing else would

126

express their intensity and their passion, and this is another fact that has contributed to the idea that Emily *must* have had a love affair. But not so. Her 'lover' of whom she speaks with such tenderness and power, was the visitation of the ideal of union with the absolute force of nature, and the ecstasy she achieved was mystical and not sexual.

This meant, of course, that she lived a double life. By day, she was the tall, competent sister who ran the house and did the chores and seemed happy with her lot — but at night, and when alone, she soared in visions from her earth-bound body, returning to it with reluctance. And as the girls had now grown out of the habit of showing each other everything they wrote, nobody ever suspected Emily's secret.

★ ★ ★

Charlotte had, in fact, already realized with much anguish that 'the infernal world' was full of dangers. Already, the longing for it and involvement in it had made her ill at Miss Wooler's school, and at twenty-five, she had decided to abandon Angria for ever — though not, of course, to give up writing other things. She wrote a sad farewell to Angria and the Angrians with whom she had lived for ten years:

'I have now written a great many books and for a long time have dwelt on the same characters and scenes and subjects ... but we must change, for the eye is tired of the picture so oft recurring and now so familiar.

'Yet ... it is no easy theme to dismiss from my imagination the images which have filled it so long; they were my friends and my intimate acquaintances ... When I depart from these I feel almost as if I stood on the threshold of a home, and were bidding farewell to its inmates ... Still, I long to quit for awhile that burning clime where we have sojourned too long — its skies flame — the glow of sunset is always upon it — the mind would cease from excitement and turn now to a cooler region where the dawn breaks grey and sober, and the coming day for a time at least is subdued by clouds.'

In other words, Charlotte was learning to live with reality. She was turning her back on imaginative fantasy and was preparing to face the world. And soon, good came of her decision, for, while pondering on the facts

128

that made them all have to split up to work and earn their daily bread, a brilliant idea occurred to her. She and Anne were both 'governessing' which they hated because it separated them from home and family, but what if they were to open a school of their own? That way, they could still make a living — and all be together.

'It will be the ideal solution,' she enthused, as soon as she arrived home on a three weeks' leave in the summer of 1841, when a family conclave was held to discuss the plan. 'Surely you must all agree? I know I've missed seeing Anne, as she had her leave earlier than mine, but I'll write to her. She's got nothing to lose. It'll only be the same work she's doing now — but if we could be doing it somewhere all together — oh, it would be paradise.'

'What do you think, Emily?' asked Papa, turning to where Emily sat silent in her corner.

'I'm happy enough here,' returned Emily slowly. 'I don't really want to leave, but if it would make the others happy — I'll go.'

Papa and Aunt exchanged looks, and Papa rubbed his chin cautiously.

'Well, it seems a sound enough plan — '

'I'll make you a proposition, Charlotte,' said Aunt, in a brisk tone. '*If* you can secure a suitable place for your school and *if* you can guarantee pupils before we risk any money, then I will advance you some of the necessary cash out of my savings.'

'Oh, Aunt — !' Charlotte was too staggered to say more.

'A loan, mind,' said Aunt, with a little smile.

'Oh, but of course, dear, dear Aunt. I shall set out about finding all we'll need to know straight away! I thought the sea-coast would be a good place for a school — perhaps Burlington. I'll write and ask Ellen — her sister Ann will know whether there's room for another school there — oh, Aunt, you've saved us all from having to go out and earn our bread amongst strangers.' And, overcome with happiness and eagerness to get on with the task in hand, as well as a sudden flood of emotion towards her aunt, Charlotte went, a little blunderingly, from the room.

Emily, though it would tear out her heart to leave her beloved moors, resigned herself to the prospect of a school, for she knew how unhappy Anne and Charlotte were in their relative positions as governesses, and, as Ellen had once noted, Emily was a lovable person and extremely generous by nature. So she put the happiness of her sisters first, and wrote in her birthday note at the end of July (the birthday notes that she exchanged with Anne, to be opened four years later):

'A scheme is at present in agitation for setting us up in a school of our own; as yet nothing is determined, but I hope and trust that it may go on and prosper and answer our highest expectations. This day four years I wonder whether we shall still be dragging out in our present condition or established to our hearts' content. Time will show. I guess at the time appointed for the opening of this paper we, i.e. Charlotte, Anne and I, shall be all merrily seated in our own sitting-room in some pleasant and flourishing seminary, having just gathered in for the midsummer ladyday. Our debts will be paid off, and we shall have cash in hand to a considerable amount. Papa, Aunt and Branwell will either have been or be coming to visit us. It will be a fine warm summer evening . . . and Anne and I will perchance slip out into the garden for a few minutes to peruse our papers. I hope either this or something better will be the case.'

Anne too expressed cautious hopes that all would go well with the school plan in her note written on Emily's birthday, while Charlotte was busier than ever, knowing nothing about setting up a school but determined to find out as soon and as much as possible.

She wrote to Ellen, asking whether Ellen thought £150 would be enough to establish a respectable — but not a *showy* — school, for she thought Aunt would not sink more than about £150 into the venture. None of them wanted to get into debt, and they did not care how humble and modest their beginnings were, just as long as the school would flourish safely.

A difficulty arose, however. It began to occur to the girls that they had no qualifications, no diplomas in music or languages, nothing, in fact, that might attract pupils to their school. Despair set in — and at this point, Charlotte heard from her friend from the Roe Head days, Mary Taylor, who was visiting her sister Martha, currently at a finishing-school just outside Brussels. She told Charlotte of the wonders of travel, of continental life, of the stimulating experiences she had had, and Charlotte felt herself lifted in the powerful grip of imagination.

'Mary's letters spoke of some of the pictures and cathedrals she had seen,' she wrote to Ellen. ' — pictures the most exquisite — and cathedrals the most venerable. I hardly know what swelled to my throat as I read her letter: such a vehement impatience of restraint and steady work; such a strong *wish for wings — wings such as wealth can furnish; such an urgent thirst to see, to know, to learn; something internal seemed to expand boldly for a minute. I was tantalised with the consciousness of faculties unexercised, — then all collapsed and I despaired . . . '*

Charlotte had already had an offer from Miss Wooler, to whom she had written for advice, that she and her sisters might revive the school at Dewsbury Moor, but her employers, the Whites, suggested an even better idea. There were so many academies flourishing in Yorkshire, they said.

'Why not postpone your project, my dear, and further your education on the Continent for a little while?' proposed Mrs White kindly. 'Then you will be able to announce a prospectus including French, German and perhaps even Italian, and you will have been continentally educated. You would stand a much better chance of gaining pupils.'

Charlotte immediately saw the sense in this — as well as the fact that it fitted in so well with her own wishes and longings after reading Mary's letters. But who was to pay for their stay on the continent? Taking her courage in both hands, Charlotte wrote to Aunt Branwell, explaining just why this project would make their school plan much more assured of success, and asking Aunt to finance herself and Emily for half a year abroad, assuring her that her money would be well spent and her loan repaid all the sooner. She was carried away with enthusiasm, and had already found out all the details about education in Brussels.

'These are advantages which would turn to vast account, when we actually commence a school,' she wrote, 'and if Emily could share them with me, only for a single half-year, we could take a footing in the world afterwards which we can never do now. I say Emily instead of Anne; for Anne might take her turn at some future period, if our school answered. I feel certain . . . that you will see the propriety of what I say; you always like to use your money to the best advantage; you are not fond of making shabby purchases; when you do confer a favour, it is often done in style; and depend upon it £50 or £100, thus laid out, would be well employed.

'Of course, I know no other friend in the world to whom I could apply on this subject except yourself. I feel an absolute conviction that, if this advantage were allowed us, it would be the making of us

134

*for life. Papa will perhaps think it a wild
and ambitious scheme; but who ever rose
in the world without ambition? When he
left Ireland to go to Cambridge University,
he was as ambitious as I am now. I want us
all to go on. I know we have talents, and I
want them to be turned to account. I look
to you, aunt, to help us. I think you will
not refuse. I know, if you consent, it shall
not be my fault if you ever repent your
kindness.'*

And Aunt did not refuse. She agreed to
the loan, and Charlotte was overjoyed, but
Emily objected to the plan. She had agreed to
Burlington, but this was altogether different,
and she said, 'It isn't fair to Anne — she's
always left out of everything.'
'But think, Emily — she's already in a
position, earning a salary. Her turn will
come later,' soothed Charlotte, forgetting
that Emily was always reluctant to leave
home, while Anne would have delighted in
the chance to travel.
'Well, I won't go and leave her alone,
slaving away. If I do go, she must have the
chance to come home,' declared Emily, and
Charlotte agreed, so Emily was committed.
But Anne's employers at Thorp Green were
reluctant to let her go, they valued her

too highly, so Anne undertook to carry on cheerfully with her work there, even though she might have come home instead.

Hasty preparations were put under way. A suitable school was found for them with the help of the British Consul in Brussels and Mr Jenkins, the Episcopalian minister there. Mr Brontë himself announced that he would accompany his daughters abroad, and the date set for their departure was 8th February 1842. The girls waded through mountains of sewing in preparation for the great event.

Mary Taylor and her brother, Joe, who were also going back to Belgium, offered to accompany the little party also, and on the morning of the appointed day, Emily said a silent goodbye, with a last longing look in the direction of her home, as she set off with Charlotte and her father for Leeds, where they were to catch the 9 a.m. train for London.

7

'I propose,' announced Monsieur Heger expansively, 'to spare you grammatical exercises and learning vocabularies; you are adults, not children. I will read to you instead passages from some of our great French authors and their masterpieces — biographical, descriptive, poetical, Mademoiselles — and then, we will consider their points of style, and adopt these for an original composition of your own on a subject of your choice.'

Charlotte was all eagerness, her eyes shone. Already she was impressed by the little, fiery man, the husband of the principal of their school, who, as a visiting teacher, took the French language and literature classes.

'What do you think of my plan?' he asked benignly.

'It sounds exciting, Monsieur,' said Charlotte, but Emily was frowning.

'I don't think it will do any good at all. It will crush all originality or thought and expression if we are trying to copy somebody else's style.'

Monsieur Heger's eyes opened wide, and he ran his hands through his hair. It was most unusual for any of his young lady pupils to contradict him.

'So!'

'Well, you asked what I thought,' said Emily calmly.

Monsieur Heger stared at her consideringly. He did not quite know what to make of this tall, lanky English girl with her unfashionable dresses with their gigot sleeves (to which Emily was partial) and her long drooping skirts. Her eyes looked back at him, large, beautiful and inscrutable, and for a moment he fell under the spell of her rare and unique mind.

'Nevertheless, Mademoiselles, I insist that we try it,' he said firmly, pulling himself together. Charlotte was watching, horrified.

'Very well, Monsieur. If you say so,' said Emily, and gave the slightest shrug.

And so they settled to their task, Charlotte willingly, Emily with a dogged determination to master her language, for she was dedicated to only one thing here in Brussels — to learn. That was what she had come here for, and she turned her mind into the one channel, unlike Charlotte, who was prepared to enjoy the novelty of being a pupil again rather than a teacher, and was enchanted with their new life at school.

The academy chosen for them was the

Pensionnat Heger, described as the 'Maison d'Education Pour les Jeunes Demoiselles sous la direction de Madame Heger-Parent', and it was situated in the Rue d'Isabelle in Brussels. Charlotte had written to the principal, enquiring about terms, for Aunt could not afford to send them to an expensive school, and Monsieur Heger recorded later that he and his wife had been so impressed by the earnestness and simplicity of Charlotte's letter that they had said to each other, 'These are the daughters of an English pastor of moderate means, anxious to learn with an ulterior view of instructing others, and to whom the risk of additional expense is of great consequence. Let us name a specific sum, within which all expenses shall be included.' So the girls were accepted at the school for the fee of £26 per annum, and did not have to pay any of the usual extras for such lessons as drawing, dancing or music.

Their journey to Brussels had been one of delight for Charlotte. She had seized their three days of sightseeing in London with all the enthusiasm of an explorer in unexplored territory, wanting to see everything. She enthused over all the masterpieces, the pictures and buildings they managed to see, and Mary Taylor watched indulgently, but Emily always made up her own mind about what she thought, and did not accept popular opinion or the opinions of others. She formed her own impressions.

They sailed for Ostend on the 12th February, and went by diligence across the Flemish countryside to Brussels, arriving in the evening two days later. The night was spent at a hotel, and in the morning, the party split up. Fond farewells were taken of Mary Taylor and Joe; and Mr Brontë and the girls, escorted by Mr and Mrs Jenkins, the friendly British Chaplain and his wife, presented themselves at the school with which Charlotte and Emily were to become so familiar. After they had been received by Madame Heger, Mr Brontë left them to settle in, and spent a few days sightseeing in the company of the Jenkinses. He returned to pay a last visit to the Pensionnat Heger to make sure his daughters were well and happy, then departed for England, and the two girls were on their own, strangers in a strange land.

Charlotte took to her new life like a duck to water, but Emily had only one thought in mind. She had come here, at Charlotte's insistence, to learn, and that was what she did. Charlotte wrote to Ellen that 'Emily works like a horse' — as indeed Emily would have needed to do, for all their lessons were conducted in French — but whereas Charlotte, though shy, was more than ready to absorb new impressions and the beauties of Brussels, Emily shut her eyes completely to everything around her, and concentrated on her studies. She never, during all the time she was in the city, spoke a single word to anyone other than her teachers, her pupils (for she later gave music lessons) and of course, Mary and Martha Taylor and Charlotte.

As they wandered in the large garden with all the sounds of the city around them when their studies were over for the day, Emily, much the taller, would lean heavily on Charlotte's arm and allow herself to speak of home.

'I hope Keeper is not pining for me too much' — talking of her great mastiff, whom she had tamed into servility and who was devoted to her.

Or, 'Do you think Victoria and Adelaide and Hero are all right?' — referring to their two tame geese and a merlin hawk Emily had rescued from the heights.

And most of all, 'I wonder how the moors are looking today.'

And she would sigh, while Charlotte pressed her arm, but wisely said nothing.

But this time, Emily's health did not give way under the strain of parting from her home and the moors. She had Charlotte, for one thing, and for another, she was determined with all her willpower to make a success of their venture into school life for the sake of Aunt Branwell, who had so generously made it possible for them to have this opportunity. She concentrated fiercely on her work, impressing Monsieur Heger so that he said later of Emily that she had a head for logic and a capability for argument unusual in a man, and very rare in a woman.

'*She should have been a man,*' *was his comment. '* — *a great navigator. Her powerful reason would have deduced new spheres of discovery from the knowledge of the old; and her strong, imperious will would never have been daunted by opposition or difficulty; never have given way but with life.*'

He also sensed the immensity of her imagination, and added,

'*Her faculty of imagination was such that, if she had written a history, her view of the scenes and characters would have been so vivid, and so powerfully expressed, and supported by such a show of argument, that it would have dominated over the reader, whatever might have been his previous opinions, or his cooler perceptions of its truth.'*

The scribbling that had kept Gondal going all these years was beginning to bear fruit in Emily's powerful style, and a judgement that applied well to the work that she *did* write — not a history, but a novel — was expressed here by a man who was fully qualified to comment. Later readers who read *Wuthering Heights* were carried before it as though a tide bore them along, and although in 'cooler' moments, many critics pronounced it melodramatic and unbelievable, when reading it, they could not escape from its overwhelming spell, and not but believe every word that they read. Once having read *Wuthering Heights*, a person was never the same again. Emily created an experience, not a book.

The girls kept very much to themselves, not caring to mix with the other chattering, giggling, Catholic continental young ladies who made up the rest of the school. They even found it difficult to mingle with their own kind. Mrs Jenkins, wife of the British Chaplain, had extended a standing invitation to Sunday dinner, and at first, Charlotte and Emily went, out of a sense of duty, but the Jenkins family overwhelmed them. Charlotte spoke only in monosyllables, and Emily never said a word. Sunday dinners were agonizing experiences, so eventually, Mrs Jenkins stopped inviting them, greatly to the relief of all concerned.

★ ★ ★

Brussels made a powerful impression on Charlotte, so that it later became the setting for two of her novels, but Emily still ground her teeth and kept at her work, though pining all the time for home. The months went on, the 'half-year' that had originally been set for their stay passed by, and still they were in Brussels. Madame had made them an offer. She would dismiss her English teacher and Charlotte should teach English instead, while Emily should give music lessons to some of the pupils. In return, they were offered free board, and the chance to continue their French and German studies.

Charlotte wrote to Ellen, when telling of Madame's proposal.

'I am inclined to accept it . . . I don't deny I sometimes wish to be in England or that

I have very brief attacks of home-sickness; but on the whole I have borne a very valiant heart so far; and I have been happy in Brussels, because I have always been fully occupied with the employment that I like. Emily is making rapid progress in French, German, music and drawing. Monsieur and Madame Heger begin to recognise the valuable parts of her character, under her singularities.'

And so they stayed. Emily gave piano lessons to some new English girls at the school, but she was unpopular with her pupils. They thought her ungainly and badly dressed, and when they tried to joke with her, teasing her about her clothes, she always said curtly, 'I wish to be as God made me.'

Then she would shut her lips firmly and say no more.

She refused to take her smaller pupils during her own study hours, and insisted on giving them their lessons during their playtime, which naturally did not endear her to them. She was also disliked because she clung so much to Charlotte, with whom the English girls wanted to make friends, so they looked on her as a spoilsport for keeping Charlotte from them, never understanding her motives in keeping her study hours sacred to study, nor why she had to cling to Charlotte for help and support in this difficult and alien land so far from her moors.

The long vacation passed, and next 'half' began at the Pensionnat Heger, and it looked as though Charlotte and Emily would be there for many more months to come, but fate was to decree otherwise. Tragedy was looming to descend and darken their lives. First of all came the news from home that Willy Weightman, who had flirted with them and enlivened their existence with the famous Valentines as well as his own particular brand of charm, was ill with cholera. Branwell, his close companion and friend, had the sad task of watching at his bedside and seeing him die in anguish and pain, on 6th September at the age of twenty-eight. It was a great blow to Branwell, who sobbed heartbrokenly throughout the funeral oration his father gave for the spirited young curate, and naturally, it was a great shock to Charlotte and Emily when they heard the news.

Yet another shock was to come very shortly. Martha, the lively, attractive sister of Mary Taylor, who had been one of Charlotte's closest friends since the Roe Head days, was still a pupil at an exclusive finishing school just outside Brussels. Martha was the pet of the family, and a charming young lady of twenty-three, but on 23rd September, she suddenly fell ill with dysentery, vomiting and chills. Again it was the dreaded cholera. Mary, who was also in Brussels, wrote to tell Charlotte that Martha was ill, but before Charlotte and Emily could make the journey the next afternoon to see her, they learned that Martha had died in the night.

The darling of everyone, Martha Taylor was buried in the Protestant cemetery outside Brussels, and on 30th October, Charlotte and Emily walked the six miles there and back with Mary to visit her grave. Mary showed great calmness and restraint, and Emily respected her for it, for she was forming her own ideas about death, but Charlotte found it difficult to understand why there were no frenzied outbursts of grief. Mary was a stoic, and Emily understood the depth of her feeling for her lost sister, though she did not speak of it or show it.

With these two deaths, their carefree schooldays were over now for good — but there was still more tragedy to come. Two days after their visit to Martha's grave, the girls had a letter from home telling them that Aunt Branwell was seriously ill. It was urgent. They must return at once. They told the Hegers, and began to pack frantically, but the next morning, before they could even finish their packing, another letter came containing the news of Aunt's death. She had died on 29th October.

Sad and dispirited, they continued with their plans for returning home, even though they realized they would be too late for the funeral. Emily left the Pensionnat Heger gladly — she was never to see it again, but Charlotte, unknowing to herself, was already half-longing to return, for something had happened to her. She was falling in love with Monsieur Heger, and the thought that this might be goodbye for ever was not to be borne. Sublimely unaware of her feelings, Monsieur Heger wrote a letter to be carried home to Mr Brontë, to be read and considered when the family grief and pain had settled a little. Charlotte hoped, as Madame saw them off on the steam packet at Antwerp, that she would return, but Emily had already decided that for her, the parting was final.

* * *

The girls arrived home to find a house in the aftermath of mourning, grief and tragedy. The worst of it had fallen upon Branwell, who, just before they sailed for Brussels, had been dismissed from his position with the railways at Luddenden Foot, and had come home to suffer a severe breakdown which bordered on the insane. Branwell was never a fighter, and his bitterness and failure were more than he could bear. While Charlotte and Emily were fighting their own battles in Brussels, Branwell was wallowing in a wave of illness and depression.

But, as with all the family, the peace of the Parsonage slowly mended his wounded pride and lacerated heart, and soon he was himself again. Actually, the swing of his spirits from zero up to the heights spoke of mental troubles, for Branwell was prone to increasing hysteria and unbalance of mind, but no one suspected that at a time when mental illness had scarcely been recognized as such. He began to write again, and was soon absorbed in Angria — Charlotte may have tried to break away from it, but Branwell never did, and as well as his writing, he found great pleasure during that summer while the girls were at Brussels, with Willy Weightman, with whom he would go shooting and walking, exercising his mind and body in healthy pastimes.

Then came Mr Weightman's illness of cholera. He was only a year older than Branwell, and his death came as a terrible shock to the young man, who wrote to an acquaintance, 'I have had a long attendance at the deathbed of the Revd. William Weightman, one of my dearest friends.' He was crushed and numbed by the blow.

In Thorp Green, where she was still cheerfully and loyally slaving at her 'governessing', Anne too, was stricken, for she had loved Mr Weightman, though her love had never been returned, and she wrote a tragic little memorial poem in his memory:

'Life seems more sweet that thou didst
   live,
And men more true that thou wert
   one;
Nothing is lost that thou didst give,
Nothing destroyed that thou hast done.'

She never forgot him.

Meanwhile, the news came of Martha Taylor's death in Brussels, a second blow that weakened Branwell's faith in God — or indeed, helped to point out to him that there was no God at all. And, finally, with Willy Weightman scarcely buried, Aunt Branwell fell ill, and to Branwell again came the burden of watching her suffer and die, for Mr Brontë, unable to help, remained in his study in prayer.

In the same letter to his acquaintance, Francis Grundy, a railway engineer with whom he had worked, in which he had described Willy Weightman's death, Branwell wrote,

'And now I am attending at the deathbed of my aunt, who has been for twenty years as my mother. I expect her to die in a few hours . . . ' And when Aunt did die he scribbled: 'I am incoherent, I fear, but I have been waking two nights witnessing such agonising suffering as I would not wish my worst enemy to endure; and I have now lost the guide and director of all the happy days connected with my childhood . . . '

Life at the Parsonage had been torn in two, and the real tragedy of Aunt's death was that she had died of 'exhaustion from constipation', a condition which in these days might appear trivial, but which in those days was fatal. Never again would she swish about the house in her silk dresses, laughing as she presented her snuff-box and invited, 'A pinch of snuff, ha?'

Never again would the click of her pattens be heard going into the kitchen, or her voice upraised in protest at the dogs coming into the house. Aunt Branwell was gone for ever.

The family rallied round poor, stricken Branwell. Anne obtained leave of absence from Thorp Green and arrived home, but only reached it in time for the funeral, while Charlotte and Emily raced across the continent, eventually coming, tired and travel-weary, to the Parsonage door when everything was over. The funeral had been held some days before, and the house though shaken was superficially calm again. Even Branwell seemed calm too, though in his soul, he had been horrified and terrified by these two further brushes with the final enemy of all — death. The faces of Maria and Elizabeth were revived in his memory, and the agonized eyes of his aunt as she cried out for release from her pain tore at his heart. He knew that he himself would never be able to fight when the time came. There was only one answer — escape in drink and drugs. This was engraved now on Branwell's mind, though to all outward appearances, he was as self-possessed as anyone could possibly be under such circumstances.

The time had obviously come for the girls and Branwell to decide what was to be done with regard to changes in the household now that Aunt was gone. What were their future plans to be? Her small possessions had been divided up between them, and the girls had each received the sum of about £350, which meant that they possessed more money than they had ever had in their lives before, and ensured their personal independence, but this made little difference with regard to their immediate prospects. Branwell had been left no money, for Aunt, when making her will some years before had believed, in common with the rest of the family, that he was destined for great things and could make his own way in the world.

Anne was still needed at Thorp Green, where her employers thought much of her, and she decided to return to her 'governessing', though the possession of her little windfall meant that she would never have to go out under duress as a governess again. She chose to carry on with her pupils, and even managed to obtain a post for Branwell, newly-quiet and self-contained, as tutor for her employers' son Edmund. So after Christmas both Anne and Branwell departed for Thorp Green.

Charlotte still had the vision of a school of their own in mind, but was torn by her longing to return to her 'master', Monsieur Heger. This was made possible for her by Monsieur's letter to Mr Brontë, which praised the efforts of both girls he had taught in Brussels, and continued that it would be a tragedy for them to give up their studies and training as teachers at this point. He offered to give one or both of them a teaching position for the coming year — and Charlotte was eager to return and take up the opportunity. Not only would it mean she would see her beloved 'master' again, but the experience would be of inestimable value when they came to open their own school. So Charlotte returned to Brussels, leaving Emily to take care of the household and look after Papa, whose eyesight was failing.

Emily was in her element. She was in complete control of the Parsonage at last, and the legacy from her aunt meant that she would never have to leave again. She was home for good, and the only shadow across her gladness — apart from her natural sorrow at her aunt's death — was the fact that while she had been away, some of her pets, the tame geese and her merlin hawk, Hero, had been got rid of. She mourned them, and turned for comfort to Keeper her great mastiff, who was overjoyed at her return, taking fresh hope and energy to renew her spirits after her exile by long tramps across the moors in Keeper's company, and running the household with contented efficiency. She also showed considerable acumen in investing the money of all the girls in the York and North Midland Railway Company, and displayed a very good head for business in this direction. She settled down to a life that was full of hard work, little or no outside distractions — and her dreams. Her cup was full; she could ask for no more, as she gave herself up once again to her visions.

★ ★ ★

She was like a rock, and everyone in the household came to her when in difficulties. On one occasion, she parted Keeper and another great dog from the village who were fighting, by shaking the pepper-pot in their faces, while a group of men stood by, afraid to interfere. She learned to shoot Papa's pistols, so that, as her father's eyesight failed, she would be able to defend the family and Parsonage if necessary. Her father called her his right hand, the very apple of his eye, and indeed she was, as blindness came creeping up on him.

Her visions came back in full measure, and she wrote prolifically, trying to communicate her feeling of unity with nature, and reaching out to a new freedom of spirit, but bound to earth by her sense of pity for the misery of humanity, and her sense of compassion for the human condition. Her mind was forming theories that she would put to good use when she came to write *Wuthering Heights* — theories about heaven and hell, about death, about love, a love that could last for a lifetime and overcome both life and death itself.

She and her father became very close during the months they passed together in the quiet of the Parsonage. He believed in freedom of thought, and respected Emily's privacy and the secrecy of her mental activities. She would play the piano, and he would sit in the twilight world of his growing blindness and listen, for she played with a brilliant and excellent touch. Indeed, after her death, the little piano upset him so much that he could not bear to think she would never play it again, and had it taken from his study and put upstairs where he need never look at it.

Time passed, and more than a year later, in January 1844, Charlotte came home from Brussels, armed with parting gifts from the Hegers of books and a Teaching Diploma from the Athénée Royal. She also brought back with her, though she tried hard to fight it off, a bruised heart and a hopeless love for Monsieur Heger that was to haunt her for two long years. What had happened to her in Brussels? She had returned to her 'master', but Madame Heger had seen what was happening, that the unsophisticated English Miss had become more attached to her husband than was reasonable or permissible. He himself was unaware of this, and Madame made sure that he remained so. And she set herself, in a cool and calculated manner, to keep her husband separated from Charlotte, and to drive Charlotte from the school. Poor Charlotte became more and more bewildered and unhappy. As a teacher and not a pupil, she now saw next to nothing of Monsieur Heger, and surely Madame's manner had changed? She had always been friendly — had that friendliness turned to coolness? But why? For Charlotte herself did not realize that her feeling for her 'master' was love, only that she needed to see him and speak to him as she needed air in order to breathe.

She suffered months of misery, and at last decided to leave, crushed and hopeless, but unable to bear the situation any longer. She had no notion that she was sexually in love, and would have been horrified to put such an idea into words — but it was there just the same, and it was with spirits at a very low ebb indeed that Charlotte returned home.

She hoped to find stimulation and consolation at the Parsonage, but instead, she found her father suffering increasingly from cataracts, half-blind and a shadow of his former self, dependent on Emily, who was wrapped up in her dream world to such an extent that, though Charlotte did not know it, she had begun to collect her poems in two notebooks, as though aware now of the value of what she was doing. One book she titled 'Emily Jane Brontë. GONDAL POEMS' and in the other she copied the best of her purely personal work. Both were kept in strict secrecy.

Anne and Branwell were home for the Christmas holidays, and Charlotte, anxious to occupy her mind with something other than the thought of her parting from her 'master', broached the idea of opening their school.

'But I suppose we could not leave Papa now,' she said regretfully, and for the present, the prospect of the 'Misses Brontës' Establishment' was reluctantly abandoned. Anne and Branwell returned to Thorp Green, and Charlotte was left alone with Emily, her father and the servants. She suffered from boredom and her own private sorrow and found no comfort in the house that had previously held such joy for her. Instead, the silent walls seemed to imprison her rather than offer comfort.

Eventually, in the spring during a spell of fine weather when they could wander on the moors, she began to tell Emily her tale of woe. The agony of parting from her beloved 'master', the fact that though she had written eagerly to him, he did not reply to her letters. Was Madame intercepting them? Emily listened with sympathy. Her own heart was free, but both her sisters were suffering from unrequited love — Anne because the man she loved was dead, and Charlotte because the object of her affection was married to another. And nothing could be done to help either of them.

A restless spring passed into summer. Charlotte still wrote her pathetic letters to Monsieur Heger, and endured the agony of his reluctance to reply and his coolness when he did so. She tried hard to occupy her mind, and by the time of the summer holidays, when Anne and Branwell were home once more, she had thought of something into which she could throw her energies, something to sustain her.

'We can't go away to open a school and leave Papa, that's certain, but why don't we open one here? Convert the house and take pupils here at the Parsonage? Oh, don't you see? That would be the answer to everything.'

Emily, not wanting her privacy intruded upon, refused to teach, but offered to look after the heavy housework that would inevitably accompany the presence of young lady boarders at the Parsonage; and the others were enthusiastic. Ellen, who was staying with them, was drawn into the plan, and said she would try to get them pupils. Charlotte threw herself heart and soul into the project, drawing up a syllabus and having copies printed to be circulated amongst all her friends and acquaintances.

But alas! Again her hopes were dashed. Not one pupil materialized, and in October, Charlotte wrote to Ellen:

'I, Emily and Anne are truly obliged to you for the efforts you have made on our behalf, and if you have not been successful you are only like ourselves. Everyone wishes us well, but there are no pupils to be had. We have no present intention, however, of breaking our hearts on the subject, still less of feeling mortified at defeat.'

But by November, the true reality of the situation had come home to Charlotte, and she told Ellen cynically, 'Depend upon it, if you were to persuade a mamma to bring her child to Haworth, the aspect of the place would frighten her, and she would probably take the dear girl back with her instanter.'

Emily remained a silent, but sympathetic companion in the background of Charlotte's dashed hopes and growing despair — for she was still suffering the loss of her 'master', and it comforted her a little to talk to Emily about him. Emily had such willpower of her own that she could have fought off any similar happening to herself, but she had to stand by and watch Charlotte becoming more and more depressed as the year passed, and Anne, too, grew bitter and rebellious with her life at Thorp Green. Emily was the rock they clung to in their need, Charlotte with her increasing obsession with the 'master' who would not respond to her letters and Anne in her hopeless longing for Willy Weightman and the misery of her governess' life.

Emily herself felt she was lucky. Both her sisters were suffering, but she had her inner world, 'the world within' into which she could escape.

'So hopeless is the world without,' she
  wrote,
The world within I doubly prize;

161

Thy world where guile and hate and
doubt
And cold suspicion never rise;
Where thou and I and Liberty
Have undisputed sovereignty.'

The following year, Charlotte's friend Mary Taylor emigrated to New Zealand, and before she went, tried to persuade Charlotte to look elsewhere for new friends and interests, and not stagnate at Haworth.

'You could teach anywhere now, Charlotte. Abroad on the continent, or even come to New Zealand with me. I hate to see you so melancholy.'

Charlotte was silent, then she said sadly, 'I'm sorry — I don't really want to stay on at home, my health isn't good there, and my eyesight has been bad, but I don't think I would feel any different with just a change of surroundings. It might do for some people, but not for me.'

Mary, of course, did not know what it was that had broken her friend's spirit, nor of the obsessional love that kept her awake at nights and haunted her dreams when she finally slept.

'But if you carry on like this, think what you'll be like in five years time,' Mary protested, but the expression on

Charlotte's face made her break off. 'Don't cry, Charlotte!'

Charlotte did not cry, but she said miserably, 'I have to stay.'

Anne too was finding life too difficult for her to cope with, and that summer, she gave in her notice to her employers, the Robinsons, and left Thorp Green to come home for good. She and Emily were reunited, and in their pleasure, even undertook a trip as far as York in June.

'Though the weather was broken, we enjoyed ourselves very much,' Emily wrote in her birthday diary paper.

But all was not well at the Parsonage. Charlotte was gloomy and discontented.

'I can hardly tell you how time gets on here at Haworth,' she had written to Ellen earlier in the year. *'There is no event whatever to mark its progress — one day resembles another — and all have heavy, lifeless physiognomies — Sunday — baking-day and Saturday are the only ones that bear the slightest distinctive mark — meantime life wears away — I shall soon be thirty — and I have done nothing yet — Sometimes I get melancholy — at the prospect before and behind me — yet it is wrong and foolish to repine — and*

undoubtedly my duty directs me to stay at home for the present — There was a time when Haworth was a very pleasant place to me, it is not so now — I feel as if we are all buried here.'

More trouble was to come, however. Branwell, returning home for the summer holidays, received a letter from his employer dismissing him in extremely unflattering terms, and implying that he had been having a love affair with Mrs Robinson. On receiving the letter, Branwell collapsed mentally and physically, and spent nights of sleeplessness in horror and shame, remaining shattered by what had come to light, and causing a great deal of trouble for his sisters with his drinking and drugs and ravings. Mr Robinson had threatened that he was not to communicate again with the woman he loved! He could not bear it!

The family soon decided that it was the lady who had been the seducer, not Branwell, who was the younger by seventeen years, but, suffering silently from tragic loves of their own, the girls had little sympathy for Branwell's hysterical behaviour — all except Emily, who had worked out her theory of pity for man's weakness and realized that a person cannot act out of character. Charlotte despised him for his lack of willpower and washed her hands of him. Gentle Anne, who had seen all too much of what went on in the Robinson household, prayed for his soul.

Then, during the autumn of 1845, Charlotte made a discovery that was to change their whole lives.

8

Charlotte and Emily faced each other across Emily's little writing-desk, which stood open. Charlotte held Emily's book of *Gondal Poems* in her hand. They were engaged in a bitter quarrel.

'You had no right to pry into my private papers,' said Emily, steely-faced.

'I'm sorry, Emily, but the desk was open. I couldn't help myself. I only glanced at first — ' Charlotte tried to soothe her sister, but her heart was racing, her face shone with enthusiasm as she grasped the book.

'You didn't just glance. You've read all my Gondal poems while I was in the kitchen, you've just told me, and they are meant to be private,' said Emily, her stillness like that of a cornered animal. 'Give the book back to me this minute.'

'But Emily — let me try to explain.'

'I don't want any explanations. I just want my book back, and I don't want to hear another word about my work. Those poems are my secret writing, not for anyone else to read, not even you,' interrupted Emily furiously, holding out her hand. 'Give me the book.'

'I can't just let it pass, Emily. They're too good, too great for that. They're — why, they're works of genius. You should be proud of them,' said Charlotte, her face flushed eagerly. 'Truly, they are. The poetry is condensed and terse, vigorous and — and genuine. They're not like anything I've ever read before. They're full of music, wild strange music. They should be published . . . '

'Never!' The explosive word burst from Emily's lips.

'Please, Emily. You'll never know how it uplifted me to read them, and I've been so downcast lately. I knew you were writing poetry, but I didn't know what. Now that I've seen them — '

'You should never have looked. I told you they were private,' said Emily curtly, and held out her hand again, 'now give me the book back.'

'No, I can't let this go. They must be published. They're even better than the poems Branwell had published in the *Halifax Guardian*; even better than the one Anne had published in *Chamber's Journal*. You know how we all wanted to be authors at one time. Well, you *are* an author, Emily.'

Charlotte was pleading now. 'Let me help you to get them published in book form. They'll be wildly successful, I'm sure.'

'I don't want them published. I want them back,' said Emily, through set teeth, 'and I never want to hear another word about publication or books. I don't want people prying into my private thoughts.'

'But you owe it to the world, Emily. Think if — if Wordsworth or somebody like that had said the same about his work — .'

'I'm not Wordsworth!' Emily seized the book and threw it into her desk. She slammed it shut and faced Charlotte trembling with the violence of her emotions. 'I'll never forgive you for prying and peering into my secret things.'

Anne had been watching the scene with large eyes, her attention flitting from one sister to the other. Now she spoke quietly.

'If you liked Emily's poems, Charlotte, perhaps you'd like to see some of mine. *I* won't mind you reading them.'

'Oh, yes. Thank you, Anne dear. I'll read them with pleasure,' said Charlotte, 'and you can read the ones I've written if you want to.'

Anne left the room, returning with a bundle of papers which she handed to Charlotte, while Emily turned away, refusing to have anything to do with what was happening. The fact that Charlotte had read her Gondal poems — the inmost expression of her secret world — had hurt her deeply.

Charlotte sat down with Anne's poems and began to read, while Anne waited for her reaction. Abruptly, Emily went out of the room. After a while, Charlotte lifted her head, settling her spectacles on her nose.

'Why, they're very good, Anne.'

'Do you think so?' asked Anne, eagerly.

'I do. They're sweet and sincere. Oh, Anne — .' And Charlotte sighed. 'If only Emily would agree to have hers published too. We always wanted to be authors and this is our chance. We might publish a volume together, all of us. It would be something really exciting to do.'

'She'll come round, I'm sure she will. It was just the suddenness of your finding her book open and reading it without her permission,' soothed Anne. Charlotte straightened her back.

'Yes, I'm determined to win her round. Why, we could make up a volume between us — .' Charlotte's mind was racing. Here at last was something she could put her heart into, something to comfort her and give her a purpose, instead of brooding on her 'master's abandonment of her and watching Branwell staggering about the house under the influence of drink or laudanum, something to take her attention away from the fact that her father's eyes were now so bad that he had been told he must have an operation for the cataracts that were darkening his world.

'I'd like that, especially if we were all involved,' said Anne quietly.

'We'll have to work on her, then. Persuade her to let us have some of her verse published,' said Charlotte. 'They really are beautiful, Anne. Like — like a great wind blowing across the moors. She *is* a genius. She has a marvellous mind and her poems are splendid, really wonderful.'

'Perhaps mine aren't good enough,' said Anne wistfully.

'Oh, yes they are. And I think my own would pass muster, though they're not half so fine as Emily's. If we could put a volume together, it would be a dream come true,' said Charlotte, fiercely resolving that at all costs, she would bring Emily round. She was filled with excitement. 'I'll persuade her somehow.'

* * *

170

Charlotte could be as stubborn as Emily. She immediately set to work to rectify the damage that had been done, apologizing in such a spirit of humility for what Emily called 'prying' that at last Emily grudgingly forgave her, but still would not agree to let anyone else see her work, and it was a week before Charlotte could persuade her to let some of her poems appear in the book of verse she was planning.

'As long as I can choose which of mine are to go in,' she compromised at length, more out of pity for Charlotte, who had suffered so many disappointments during the past two years, than because she was really interested in the project.

'But of course you can choose. We'll all make a selection of our best work,' said Charlotte joyfully. 'You won't regret it, Emily. Yours will be the best poetry in the book. Your verses will really make it a success, and you know how we've always had an ambition to be authors. We might even make some money out of it.'

'I don't care about the money,' shrugged Emily.

'No, well, that doesn't matter, but just think — to have a book published of our very own. We'll be following in Papa's footsteps.'

'You're not to tell him! I don't want anyone to know I've written these,' said Emily quickly.

'No, we won't tell anybody. In fact, we could write under pseudonyms,' said Charlotte.

'I think it would be better if we did. We might even have masculine-sounding names. You know how prejudiced people can be about women authors,' contributed Anne, practically.

A long discussion followed on what pseudonyms they should choose, and eventually Charlotte said triumphantly,

'Currer. I'll keep my own initials. Currer Bell. That sounds mannish enough, doesn't it?'

'I shall be called Acton,' said Anne. 'What about you, Emily?'

'Ennis? No, Ellis perhaps,' said Charlotte. 'Ellis Bell.'

'All right,' agreed Emily briefly.

'Currer, Ellis and Acton Bell,' pronounced Charlotte. 'Oh, Emily, even you must be a little excited about what we're going to do.'

'I'm only doing it for your sake and Anne's,' said Emily gruffly, but she could not keep a note of eagerness out of her voice. Her first violent reaction that her verses should not be published had come partly from shock at the sudden way Charlotte had read those very private manuscripts, and partly from a feeling that she was not yet ready for publication. Already the way to authorship had been partially paved for them.

Branwell had long been making efforts to get into print, and had begun to write a three-volume novel (never finished) which was called *And the Weary Are at Rest*. He had, as Charlotte had mentioned to Emily, also managed to get several of his poems published in the *Halifax Guardian*; while Anne too had not been idle. At Thorp Green, she had begun a prose tale which she originally called *Passages in the Life of an Individual* but which was later to be titled *Agnes Grey*. This was a novel based on her experiences as a governess, a new departure for her from the world of Gondal. By now, she had written over two-thirds of it, and had had a poem printed in *Chamber's Journal*. Even Charlotte herself had begun a work in which she tried to exorcise her feelings for her 'master'; it was called *The Professor*.

Emily had also been toying, though in secret, not like her sisters, with the idea of a novel, but she had not yet begun it, although the stimulus of their new venture into print caused her to make a start, and when she did begin *Wuthering Heights*, it came ready-made into her mind, the product of years of germination, and flowed steadily on throughout the autumn and winter of that year, while Charlotte, in a fever of excitement, was making efforts to get their book of poems into print.

Once she had adjusted herself to the idea of publication, Emily let herself join in the eagerness of the rest, though outwardly, she was offhand about the venture. She called the book 'those rhymes', and said that as Charlotte was the one who wanted to publish them, Charlotte must see to all the details. And Charlotte did. Under her enthusiastic guidance, all three sisters selected, edited, revised and copied the best of their work, while Charlotte began to write to publishers. After a few false starts, she applied to Messrs Chambers of Edinburgh for advice, and, following this, approached the firm of Aylott & Jones in Paternoster Row, asking if the firm would be willing to publish a book of poetry — at the authors' expense, if necessary. Now that they had Aunt's legacy, they could afford to pay.

She wrote under the name of C. Brontë, and referred to the 'Bells' in the third person throughout her correspondence with the firm, which pronounced itself willing to accept the offer. On 7th February, 1846, the manuscript of the book of verse was sent off, and the sisters spent their evenings in the parlour — now called the dining-room — discussing and debating how the book would be received, whether or not it would be a success — all the exciting questions any would-be author asks himself.

The estimated cost of the work was £31. 10s. 0d, and proofs of the manuscript arrived on 10th March. By the last week in May, the book was out. They were in print! They were authors at last! For Charlotte at least, it was a dream come true. After a long correspondence with the firm of publishers, after buying a manual on the subject of book publishing and studying it, sending messages to the firm on the subject of type and format, after debating, as publication date drew nearer and nearer, how many review copies should be sent out and how much should be spent on advertising — for the cost had already exceeded the estimate by £5, and Charlotte was frightened of spending too much — she held the book in her hand. *The poems of Currer, Ellis and Acton Bell*, a slim volume bound in dark green cloth with lettering in gilt.

What a moment for her! Yet she knew that, of the contributions in the volume, Emily's were by far the greatest. Nevertheless, she refused to be daunted by the fact that poetry was not really her metier, and in fact, all three sisters had been busy during that winter on their novels, the prospect of published authorship now uppermost in their minds. Every evening, they worked secretly in the dining-room, while Papa, unaware of what they were doing, went to bed and Branwell, lay sprawled on his own disarranged mattress, a burden to the whole household with his drinking, drugs and bemoaning of the lost love of his life.

Three months before the actual publication of the book, Charlotte had paid a visit to Ellen, but had not said a word about what the sisters were doing. On her return, she found that Branwell had managed to beg a sovereign from his father, who, blinded and helpless, still doted on his once-beloved son. With it, Branwell had got himself roaring drunk, although by now, his drinking was somewhat curtailed because the girls had agreed not to give him any money however much he whined and pleaded for it. This time, however, with Charlotte away, he had slipped through their guard, and Anne and Emily were disgusted at their brother's behaviour. Even Emily, who had been the only one prepared to hold out any hope for Branwell's improvement, now said to Charlotte angrily, 'he is a hopeless being.'

Poor Branwell had been abandoned by them all now, even the sister who had been prepared previously to try and help him. They turned instead to the prospect of their coming volume of poems and their novels, which were progressing apace. They were doing so well, in fact, that at the beginning of April (again before the publication of the poems), Charlotte had already written to their publishers, her letter reading:

'*Gentlemen — C. E. & A. Bell are now preparing for the Press a work of fiction, consisting of three distinct and uncon-nected tales which may be published either together as a work of 3 vols. of the ordinary novel size, or separately as single vols. as shall be deemed most advisable.*

'*It is not their intention to publish these tales on their own account.*

'*They direct me to ask you whether you would be disposed to undertake — after having of course by due inspection of the MS. ascertained that its contents are such as to warrant an expectation of success.*

'*An early answer will oblige as in case of your negativing the proposal — inquiry*

must be made of other Publishers — I am
Gentlemen Yrs truly
                    C. Brontë.
April 6th '46.'

These 'tales' were *Agnes Grey* by Anne,
The Professor by Charlotte and *Wuthering
Heights* by Emily, which were now almost
ready to submit to a publisher. Again, under
Charlotte's ardent leadership, the girls worked
together. How wonderful if Aylott & Jones
would publish their novels all in one volume!
But the publishers replied that they did
not publish fiction, though they provided
Charlotte with a list of others who did, and
advice on how to submit the manuscript, so
Charlotte prepared to tackle this intimidating
list, although the books, as it happened, were
not ready to be sent off until after their
volume of poems had come out.

*The Poems of Currer, Ellis and Acton
Bell* made their modest appearance in the
world, and the girls waited eagerly for the
reactions of press and public. Unfortunately,
something else happened at the very same
time which was to make their burden at the
Parsonage far greater than it already was.
Mr Robinson, the husband of Branwell's
lady-love, died, and Branwell expected to
be immediately summoned to Thorp Green

by the woman whom he adored, his beloved Lydia. When the message finally came, it was not a summons, but a trumped-up tale of how Mrs Robinson could never see him again because of a codicil in her husband's will which would lose her her inheritance if she communicated in any way with Branwell Brontë.

She was, in fact, making an effort to get rid of him for ever, but he believed the tale, and this last and greatest blow to any hopes he may still have had that his life could be a happy one, reduced him to a fit. From then on, his life was one long downhill slide from which he never recovered, and he and his behaviour became a positive torment to his father and sisters.

Meanwhile, the girls were waiting breathlessly for what the world had to say about their work. Reviews appeared in the *Athenaeum* and *The Critic* on the same day that Charlotte sent off the parcel of novels to the first of the publishers on the list Aylott & Jones had given them.

Emily was not worried about trying to publish *Wuthering Heights*. She made no protest, as in the case of her poems, and even read aloud parts of it to her sisters — as, in fact they all did with their work, as it progressed, but she could not understand

179

their strange reactions. What was horrifying or tormenting about her work? Why did they complain that certain passages in the story 'banished sleep by night and disturbed mental peace by day'? What made them shudder over the nature of her hero, Heathcliff, and her heroine, Catherine? Well, let them. Emily knew that what she was writing was original and true, and refused to alter a word.

It swept her along, the final, the triumphant culmination of all her Gondal philosophies and thoughts, her testament, the crowning achievement of all her musings and observations and theorizing, as near to the truth of what she believed about life as she could get it. It sustained her, uplifted her, relieved her soul, and when it was finished, she laid down her pen feeling drained, and as though she would never be able to write another word. *Wuthering Heights* had been the great effort of her life, and it had fulfilled her to write it.

★ ★ ★

Branwell, of course, could not be told about what the girls were doing. After the Mrs Robinson fiasco, he became a danger as well as a burden, to the rest of his long-suffering family. He could not sleep during the night, but spent the long night hours in restless tossing and turning, trying to dull his mind with whisky or laudanum. He could no longer write; he could no longer read, and because he did not sleep at night, he spent his days in lethargic stupors in his room.

One evening, Anne knocked at his door, opened it and found that he had lit a candle but his unsteady hands had let it fall, and the bed curtains were on fire. She tried to drag his unconscious body out of bed, but could not, so she ran frantically for Emily's help. Emily, always calm in an emergency, filled a bucket with water, and dashed up the stairs. She dragged Branwell out of danger, ripped down the blazing curtains and put out the fire with the water in her bucket. When the mess had been cleared up, all she said was, 'don't tell Papa.'

Inevitably, Papa came to know of the degeneration of his unhappy son, and from then onwards spent his nights with Branwell, trying as best he could to watch over him with his failing eyesight. He listened to Branwell's ravings, his torments, his threats of suicide, pleas for money and sobs of remorse, wrestling and praying for Branwell's soul.

Branwell did not thank him.

Sometimes, he muttered, after a horrific night, 'He does his best, the poor old man'; or he would say if he managed to stagger down to breakfast, 'the old man and I have had a terrible night of it.'

So it was no wonder that the delivery of parcels and the sudden increase in correspondence failed to be noticed by either Mr Brontë or his son. They had far more dreadful things to worry about. It was fortunate for the girls that they had the consolation of their book of poetry and their novels to help them through that miserable period.

The reviews of the *Poems* were on the whole encouraging. The critic of the *Athenaeum* commented on Emily's verse for its *'power of wing'*.

'A fine quaint spirit has the latter (Emily)', the review reported, *'which may have things to speak that men may be glad to hear — and an evident power of wing that may reach heights not here attempted . . .'*

The Critic even went so far as to comment: *'They in whose hearts are chords stung by Nature to sympathise with the beautiful and the true, will recognise in these compositions the presence of more genius than it was supposed this utilitarian age had devoted to the loftier exercises of the intellect.'*

Other publishers were sufficiently interested to try and find out who these 'Bell brothers' were, while Charlotte, much heartened by the reviews, sent off another £10 to the publishers to be used for advertising the book.

Emily felt heartened too, for behind the identity of 'Ellis Bell', that man-like figure, she could speak and act as she wanted to, with no fears that anyone would ever guess her identity. It gave her as much protection from reality as the creation of Gondal — and when, later, Anne and Charlotte discarded their disguise, Emily fought fiercely to retain hers, and was to do so until the end. She had long since given up facing the world on its own terms.

The outlook was promising, but after two months, when Charlotte enquired how many copies had been sold, the answer was — two! And they never sold another copy of this version of their poems, but they were not discouraged, for by now, they were waiting with great eagerness to know the eventual fate of their novels. Would this publisher accept them? No — they were returned, so Charlotte merely crossed out the name on the brown-paper wrapping of the parcel, and forwarded it to the next publisher on their list. The girls paced the dining-room with renewed hopes. Perhaps this time, they would be lucky.

But a shadow had fallen over their excitement and anticipation. Papa's eyesight was getting so bad that it had been decided to consult the advice of a specialist about his cataracts. So in August, with the fate of their novels still undetermined, Charlotte and Emily went to Manchester to make arrangements with the eminent eye surgeon, Mr William James Wilson, for Papa's dreaded operation.

Mr Wilson saw them, and listened to Charlotte's account of her father's eyes.

'H'm,' he said at last. 'I cannot tell from your description whether his eyes are ready to be operated on. I must see him myself.'

So Patrick, now turned seventy and frail, had to make the journey to Manchester too, and Mr Wilson examined him. Charlotte accompanied him this time, while Emily stayed at home to look after the household.

'He's an old man,' Mr Wilson reported to her, after his examination, 'but I think he can stand it. I'm afraid an immediate operation is necessary. Next Monday, if you can manage that. Then you will have to stay here for about a month until I can see the result and make sure all is well. I have the highest hopes, Miss Brontë.'

So Charlotte sought out clean, respectable lodgings for herself and her father, and on the following Monday, the operation was performed by Mr Wilson himself, with two surgeons in attendance. Papa had requested that Charlotte remain in the room with him throughout the ordeal, which took place without an anaesthetic, and lasted for fifteen minutes. She sat stoically, trying not to breathe, as her father bore the extraction of the cataracts, and reported later that his patience and firmness had surprised the doctors.

Afterwards, he lay in bed in a dark room. He had been forbidden to move for four days, and told not to speak unless absolutely necessary. A nurse arrived, and Charlotte worried about her comfort. She and her father could manage all right with their simple wants, but a nurse would expect more, she was convinced. Charlotte did not like her, and found her 'somewhat too obsequious' and 'not much to be trusted', but she looked after Mr Brontë well enough, leaving Charlotte to sit out the lonely hours, longing for home, and acutely miserable in the midst of strangers, constantly worrying about Papa. In addition, she developed a raging toothache, which continued to plague her throughout the rest of the summer.

When the bandages were removed, Papa pronounced that he could see, but very dimly. Mr Wilson, however, was satisfied with his progress, although Charlotte was not happy, for Papa complained that his eyes were weak and sore. He was allowed to sit up now, and to have a fire, carefully screened, in the room.

Charlotte wrote despondently to Ellen: '*Papa is still a prisoner in his darkened room — into which, however, a little more light is admitted than formerly. The nurse goes today — her departure will certainly be a relief though she is I dare say not the worst of her class . . .* '

While she worried about her father, there was yet another blow. Emily had forwarded the parcel of novels, returned yet again, and Charlotte, as usual, crossed out the old address and printed in a new one, much too innocent to realize that a long list of crossed-out addresses would reveal the fact that this was a many-times-rejected manuscript to the next publisher she sent it to. The only thing that kept up her spirits during those long, weary days while Papa lay in his darkened room, was the fact that she had begun to write a new novel.

'*Jane Eyre. Chapter One.*
'*There was no possibility of taking a walk that day — .*'

The flow of the narrative carried her along, and she wrote steadily all through the weeks until her father could return to Haworth, by which time '*the mere effort to succeed had given a wonderful zest to existence*', although she did not tell anyone of this zest, but, though she continued to write in full force, resented bitterly the path of duty that kept her chained at home, the troubles Branwell was causing and the fact that she seemed to be wasting her life.

The operation was a complete success, and once back at Haworth, some of the burden of responsibility for her father was lifted from Charlotte's shoulders. Mr Brontë's sight was so improved that he was able to take over his duties again by mid-November, and Charlotte wrote to Miss Wooler, her old headmistress, '*Now* to see him walk about independently — read, write, etc, is indeed a joyful change.'

* * *

There was no change in Branwell's behaviour, however. It grew worse, and that winter was a bitter one for all the family. The weather was very bad, and they all had colds and influenza, Anne, in particular, suffering very much from asthma, but at last spring came, and summer with it, and for the girls, a note of encouragement. In July, a firm called T. C. Newby offered to accept *Agnes Grey* and *Wuthering Heights* on condition that part of the expense was borne by the authors. But it was an acceptance. Success at last!

'The only thing is, he won't take *The Professor*, Charlotte,' Emily protested, when Charlotte tried to summon up some congratulations for her sisters. It was a bitter blow to her, but she was adamant that Anne and Emily should take advantage of this offer.

'Never mind. I'll send *The Professor* off again on its own,' she said, trying to hide her disappointment. 'I'm so pleased for the two of you.'

'I don't know whether we ought to accept,' demurred Emily, but the sight of Anne, still pale and thin after her long winter illness, decided her. Anne had said only, 'I would so like to see something of mine in print.'

And so Emily wrote to Mr Newby, accepting his offer for the publication of *Agnes Grey* and *Wuthering Heights*, while Charlotte, with *Jane Eyre* almost finished, sent off *The Professor* yet again to the firm of Smith, Elder & Co.

They rejected *The Professor*, but said they would be interested in a three-volume novel and — how fortunate — she had just finished *Jane Eyre* so she let them have that. She sent off the completed manuscript just as Anne and Emily were excitedly receiving the proof-sheets of *Agnes Grey* and *Wuthering Heights*. Soon, soon, their work would be in print, and they would be real authors — all except poor Charlotte, of course.

9

Emily and Anne were soon to discover that, if their novels had not actually fallen upon stony ground with Mr Newby, they had certainly fallen among thorns. They stood by and watched as Charlotte's star very quickly rose and eclipsed their own, shining forth with an incandescent light.

Mr Newby had driven a hard bargain. He would produce an edition of 300 copies of their book (for *Wuthering Heights* and *Agnes Grey* were to be published together) if they would forward the sum of £50, which was to be refunded when 250 copies were sold. As a matter of fact, this sum was never refunded at all, and Mr Newby continued on his fraudulent way. They were sent the first proof-sheets in August, and then he held up production. They wrote to him repeatedly, wanting to know when the volume would be coming out, but he did not reply — not, that is, until he discovered that he could make some profit out of the name 'Bell', which took place after Charlotte's *Jane Eyre* had made its way in the world.

For Charlotte received very different

treatment at Smith, Elder & Co. The manuscript of *Jane Eyre* was first read by the firm's reader, Mr William Smith Williams, who took it to the owner of the firm, Mr George Murray Smith, and suggested that he too should read it. Mr Smith took it home with him one Saturday evening, even though he intended to go riding with a friend on the Sunday. He later recorded how the book affected him,

'After breakfast on Sunday morning I took the MS. of Jane Eyre *to my little study, and began to read it. The story quickly took me captive. Before twelve o'clock my horse came to the door, but I could not put the book down. I scribbled two or three lines to my friend, saying that I was very sorry that circumstances had arisen to prevent my meeting him, sent off the note by my groom, and went on reading the MS. Presently the servant came to tell me that luncheon was ready; I asked him to bring me a sandwich and a glass of wine, and still went on with* Jane Eyre. *Dinner came; for me the meal was a very hasty one, and before I went to bed that night I had finished reading the manuscript.*

'The next day we wrote to Currer Bell accepting the book for publication . . . '

Charlotte could not believe the speed at which the publishing house moved. While Emily and Anne were still writing to Mr Newby, she had proofs of *Jane Eyre* in September, and the book appeared on 16th October, some six weeks after its acceptance. She wrote to the publishers on the 19th, thanking them for the complimentary copies that had been received and hastily hidden lest Papa or Branwell should see them.

'Gentlemen — the six copies of Jane Eyre *reached me this morning. You have given the work every advantage which good paper, clear type, and a seemly outside can supply; if it fails the fault will lie with the author; you are exempt.*

'I now await the judgement of the press and public — I am gentlemen, yours respectfully,

C. Bell.'

'My dear, have you read it? It's shattering, absolutely shattering.'

'Yes, *The Times* called it ' . . . *a remarkable production.'* Listen! *'Freshness and originality, truth and passion, singular felicity in the description of natural scenery, and in the analysis of human thought, enable this tale to stand out boldly from the rest'.'*

'I couldn't put the book down.'

'The *Westminster Review* says it's decidedly the best novel of the year.'

'Oh, I couldn't agree more, my dear. I am perfectly in accord with *Fraser's Magazine*. The critic G. H. Lewes has written: '*After laughing over the* Bachelor of the Albany, *we wept over* Jane Eyre. *This is indeed a book after our own heart . . . no such book has gladdened our eyes for a long while . . . The story is not only of singular interest, naturally evolved, unflagging to the last, but fastens itself upon your attention and will not leave you. The book closed, the enchantment continues . . .* ' I do so agree. I simply can't forget it.'

'Really? I must read it.'

'Oh, you'll be quite out of fashion if you don't my dear. Simply *everyone* is reading it. It's become quite the thing to do.'

'Even Mr Thackeray read it and wept over the love passages, I believe. He couldn't put it down either.'

'If you haven't read it, you'll be right out in the cold. Everyone who is anyone is reading it.'

Everyone — anyone — read *Jane Eyre*. While Charlotte sat, hardly daring to believe what was happening, in the modest little Parsonage, her creation swept through

Victorian England and took it by storm. It was the success story to end all success stories, and *Jane Eyre* went into a second edition in December, such was the demand for it.

★ ★ ★

It was now that Mr Newby, that astute man of business, acted. *Wuthering Heights* and *Agnes Grey* were printed, *Wuthering Heights* taking up two volumes of the customary three-volume novel form, and *Agnes Grey* the third, but even then he let Emily and Anne down. The books were shabbily produced, and none of the corrections they had made on the proof-sheets were carried out. They found this when they received their own complimentary copies in mid-December. The volumes were bound in deep claret-coloured ribbed cloth, decorated with ornamentation, and with the titles in gold lettering on the spine. But the fact that what lay within had been so carelessly produced spoiled the books for them, and Charlotte, exultant in her own success, felt deeply for their disappointment.

'The books are not well got up,' she reported to her own publishers. 'They abound in errors of the press . . . I feel painfully that

Ellis and Acton have not had the justice at Newby's hands that I have had at those of Smith and Elder.'

She tried to get them to change publishers, but in typically stubborn fashion, Emily clung to the man who had given them their chance, and Anne followed her lead. Undoubtedly, Emily was wrong to remain loyal to the 'rascal', but she was becoming increasingly intractable and simply would not take advice, however well meant.

Mr Newby played on the curiosity of all who wondered about the sudden publication so soon after *Jane Eyre* of another volume written in the name of Bell. He tried to insinuate to the public that all three novels had been written by the same person, and the result was that *Wuthering Heights* and *Agnes Grey* were believed by many to have been the product of the pen of the famous Currer Bell, and were unfairly compared to the wonderfully successful *Jane Eyre*.

The *Athenaeum*, in its review of *Wuthering Heights* and *Agnes Grey* at the end of December, personified this confusion. The critic wrote:

'Jane Eyre, *it will be recollected, was edited by Mr Currer Bell. Here are two tales so closely related in cast of thought, incident and language as to excite some curiosity. All three might be the work of one hand — but the first issued remains the best. In spite of much power and cleverness, in spite of its truth to life in the remote corners of England — Wuthering Heights is a disagreeable story. The Bells seem to affect painful and exceptional subjects — the misdeeds or oppression of tyranny, the eccentricities of 'women's fantasy'. They do not turn away from dwelling upon those physical acts of cruelty — the contemplation of which true taste rejects . . . and if the Bells, singly or collectively, are contemplating future or frequent utterances in Fiction, let us hope that they will spare us further interiors so gloomy as the one here elaborated with such dismal minuteness.'*

This, of course, was a direct attack on *Wuthering Heights*. The reviewer dismissed Anne's contribution with the words:

'In this respect, Agnes Grey is more acceptable to us, though less powerful.'

This unfortunate misunderstanding troubled all three of the sisters. Emily went about with a cold, set face, inwardly deeply hurt by the way in which her novel had been received by the press, outwardly scornful. Anne showed her hurt a little more, though they did not say much about how they felt, but the reviewers did, on the whole, reject Emily's book, and took very little notice of Anne's.

Of course, *Wuthering Heights* was beyond their comprehension. It was judged to be 'inexpressibly painful' by the *Atlas*, though the critic admitted it had 'a sort of rugged power', while adding:

'We know nothing in the whole range of our fictitious literature which represents such shocking pictures of the worst forms of humanity.'

Another reviewer wrote:

'There is not in the entire dramatis personae a single character which is not utterly hateful or thoroughly contemptible. If you do not detest a person you despise him; and if you do not despise him you detest him with your whole heart.'

One journal even went so far as to suggest 'demonaic influence', and readers were warned that they would be shocked, disgusted and sickened by the book.

It was further declared that Ellis Bell knew nothing about the art of writing novels — a hurtful criticism of Emily, who had been writing for years, and who had put the result of long months of thought and contemplation into *Wuthering Heights*. Even the reviewers who had a word of praise for the book were misguided in their judgements, showing that they had not understood a word of it, and it was received later in America in the same fashion. The *North American Review* called the hero a 'brute-demon' and described the author as 'a man of uncommon talents but dogged, brutal and morose'.

Charlotte's happiness over the success of *Jane Eyre* was almost completely destroyed. At first, she had been thrilled at its success. Even Papa had been proudly let into the secret at long last, though he later admitted he had had his suspicions that something was going on, though he did not know what.

But after the first flush of success of *Jane Eyre*, the others urged Charlotte to tell him about it, and she went into his study one afternoon, a copy of the book in her hand, and announced, 'Papa, I've been writing a book.'

'Have you, my dear?' replied Patrick, looking up from his work.

'Yes,' said Charlotte, unable to repress

her bubbling happiness, 'and I want you to read it.'

'But my dear Charlotte, I think it would try my eyes too much,' said Patrick, frowning, 'my sight is still weak, you know.'

'It isn't in manuscript, though, Papa, it's printed,' Charlotte told him, and his frown deepened.

'My dear girl! You haven't had it printed? Think of the expense — and it will almost certainly make a loss, for how will you sell it? Nobody knows you or your name.'

Charlotte positively glowed. 'I don't think it will be a loss, Papa. Look, I've brought you a copy and some reviews. Let me tell you a bit more about it.'

She read a few pieces from some of the reviews to her father, and then presented him with the copy for him to read. Later, he came out of his study and announced proudly, 'Girls, do you know, Charlotte has written a book, and it's much better than likely.'

Moments like these were worth all their hard work to the girls, and they exchanged knowledgeable and happy smiles.

★ ★ ★

But this, of course, was before Mr Newby began to spread his fraudulent rumours. Not content with trying to convince everyone that all three books had been written by the same person, he even went as far as to insinuate that the author was in fact his own Ellis Bell, and that Currer Bell had not written *Jane Eyre* at all. Charlotte wrote to her publishers with some amusement at first, assuring them that 'We are three', but later, when all the girls had become increasingly upset by Newby's behaviour, she wrote in a more anxious vein:

'*I should not be ashamed to be considered the author of* Wuthering Heights *and* Agnes Grey, *but, possessing no real claim to that honour, I would rather not have it attributed to me, thereby depriving the true authors of their just meed . . . What is meant by charges of* trickery *and* artifice *I have yet to comprehend. It is no art in me to write a tale — it is no trick in Messrs Smith and Elder to publish it. Where do the trickery and artifice lie?*'

For by now, the journals were playing a guessing game as to the authorship of the Bell books, and were making these very claims, that trickery and artifice were being used. The only trickery and artifice lay, of course, with Mr Newby, and Emily suffered a great deal from his unsavoury methods of publicizing her book. Charlotte discussed the subject at some length with Mr W. S. Williams, the reader at Smith and Elder, who had been the first to recognize the merits of *Jane Eyre*, and with whom she had now struck up a lively correspondence — without, however, giving away her identity.

'You are not far wrong in your judgement respecting *Wuthering Heights* and *Agnes Grey*,' she wrote, early on, even before the critics had begun their attacks. 'Ellis has a strong, original mind, full of strange though sombre power. When he writes poetry that power speaks in language at once condensed, elaborated, and refined, but in prose it breaks forth in scenes which shock more than they attract. Ellis will improve, however, because he knows his defects. *Agnes Grey* is the mirror of the mind of the writer.'

All of which goes to show that, even in her closeness to her sisters, Charlotte herself did not understand them. She felt that she had to apologize for Emily — for writing a masterpiece! She never really understood what the central themes of the book were — the agony of being separated from the beloved object, a love that would last for life, the power of nature to forgive and allow much for the sake of adherence to its innocent quality. Her assertion that Ellis would improve 'because he knows his defects' was quite wrong. To Emily, every word she had written was the truth, and she had no thought of improvement, just a scorn and anger for the stupidity of a world which could not recognize what she had done and chose to misunderstand it.

Charlotte's rather patronizing remark about Anne, too, showed that she, in common with others, looked on Anne as a dear, gentle soul, without giving credit to the steel beneath the velvet glove. Anne was already working on her study of drunkenness, *The Tenant of Wildfell Hall*, and was making a good job of a subject that would have dismayed most young ladies, but about which Anne felt it was her duty to write, with Branwell as a terrible, ever-present model before her eyes.

Charlotte too had begun another book, *Shirley*, and Emily was in correspondence with Mr Newby over a second novel. She had made several false starts, none of which had yet satisfied her, so she had destroyed them. *Wuthering Heights* had drained her, it seemed, but she was playing with ideas, and the obsequious Mr Newby was all too eager to snap up anything she wrote, for, as a result of his devious methods, Emily's first novel was now selling well.

Charlotte had written to Mr Williams at Smith and Elder, '*If Mr Newby always does business in this way, few authors would like to have him for their publisher a second time*', but both Emily and Anne had no intention of changing their publisher, and still stayed faithful, in spite of the way he had treated them. They had great depths of loyalty — misguided though it was. Charlotte pleaded with them in vain.

'But just look at the treatment you've had from him, Anne. Why not come to Smith and Elder? They're good, kind men. Emily? They won't trick you, or go in for scandalous rumours about the authorship of your work — and they'll pay you properly, too.'

'Mr Newby is my publisher,' replied Emily inflexibly, and Charlotte realized with sudden dismay that Emily had passed beyond the stage of taking rational advice. Indeed, she was becoming increasingly odd about being given any advice at all. Charlotte shrugged her shoulders helplessly. Emily would just have to go her own way then.

★ ★ ★

Anne too, in her quiet manner, went her own way. She was the first of the sisters to complete a second novel, and she sent it not to Smith, Elder & Co, who would have been only too pleased to act for her, but to the infamous Mr Newby, who this time offered her slightly better terms for it. So far, he had paid neither Emily nor Anne anything for their first books, but he now became magnanimous.

For *The Tenant of Wildfell Hall*, Anne was to receive £25 on delivery of the manuscript and another £25 when 250 copies were sold, and she did not have to contribute a penny herself. Set against the terms of Smith, Elder & Co, who in all paid Charlotte £500 for *Jane Eyre*, this was meagre fare indeed, but Anne was satisfied.

The Tenant of Wildfell Hall appeared in June of that year, 1848, and was an immediate success. Of course, Mr Newby could not leave well alone. He advertised the book in an ambiguous manner, suggesting yet again that all the Bell books were by the same person, and that this was a follow-up to *Jane Eyre*. Charlotte, with flaming cheeks, wrote to her publishers:

'*Newby has announced a new work by Acton Bell. The advertisement has, as usual, a certain tricky turn to its wording which I do not admire.*'

But all the same, the reviewers found *The Tenant* 'the most interesting novel which we have read for a month past', and Anne felt she had not failed in her duty. She had taken Branwell's fate very much to heart, and with her own deeply sensitive and morbid turn of mind, induced by her strict upbringing in religion by her aunt, she felt it essential to warn the world of the sin and wickedness that drink could bring about. She reaped her reward — the world heeded her, and the success of her book soothed and calmed her soul. Perhaps, after all, she had not failed to contribute something to humanity.

Mr Newby was rubbing his hands with glee. He plunged straight away into negotiations with Harper Brothers of New York, who were to bring out an American edition of *The Tenant*. Mr Newby assured them solemnly that this was actually the latest work by the famed Currer Bell, author of *Jane Eyre*, and that as far as he knew, Currer (not Ellis, this time) was in fact the author of all these highly esteemed and controversial works.

But Mr Newby was riding for a fall, for it so happened that Harper Brothers had already entered into a firm agreement with Smith, Elder & Co, for Currer Bell's next novel, which was to be *Shirley*. They informed George Smith at Smith and Elder what Newby had done, and asked him for an explanation. He naturally felt the situation to be a very delicate one. So delicate, in fact, that he wrote to Haworth asking, very tactfully, to have the matter cleared up, once and for all. Who, he wanted to know, *was* the author of *The Tenant*? Was it Currer Bell, as Mr Newby had stated? Mr Smith wrote that he 'would be glad to be in a position to contradict the statement', adding that he was quite sure in his own mind that it was quite untrue — for the firm had every confidence by now in the integrity of Currer Bell, if nothing else.

The letter caused a sensation at the Parsonage.

'It's a disgrace to Mr Smith's honour,' exclaimed Charlotte, hotly, when the girls had read it.

'And to yours, too,' added Anne, horrified by Mr Newby's behaviour. 'We really should explain, or do something, Charlotte.'

'This time Mr Newby has gone too far,' Charlotte declared. She was very angry, and there were spots of red in her cheeks. 'I've always mistrusted him. What do you think, Emily?'

Emily, who was sitting silently, looked up with a start.

'It's nothing to do with me,' she said. 'You

206

and Anne are the ones who are involved.'

'Well, I suggest that we all go up to London and make ourselves known. We can't hide behind these pseudonyms any longer if it causes such confusion to everybody,' said Charlotte.

'No!' That was Emily, of course.

'But Emily, we must,' said Anne gently. She too was greatly distressed. 'People, good people like Mr Smith are being put in the wrong because we won't tell them who we really are.'

'I shall never tell anyone,' said Emily harshly, but there was an undercurrent of fear beneath her words. This was a threatened invasion of her much-loved privacy, 'and I forbid you to tell anyone about me.'

There was silence, then Charlotte said, 'Well, you and I had better go, Anne. That way we can prove that there are at least two of us.'

'Yes, I think we shall have to,' Anne agreed, miserably. She tried once more. 'Emily, are you sure?'

'I will never reveal my identity — never!' said Emily firmly, and she turned away. 'You and Charlotte go if you want to, but I'm staying here.'

Anne looked helplessly at Charlotte, who shrugged.

'Very well, then,' Charlotte said. Really, Emily was getting odder and odder. She just could not seem to see sense. It was almost as if she was obsessed with her privacy. 'Anne, we'd better pack a few things and take the first train we can. The sooner this is cleared up the better.'

So Charlotte and Anne, with their modest boxes sent on ahead, set out that same day for London. Inwardly, Charlotte was full of excitement, though she would not admit it even to herself, but she had always secretly wanted to reveal her true identity and be recognized for what she was, her true personality. Now was her chance.

They left after tea, had to walk through a thunderstorm to the station, arrived at Leeds and took the night train to London, discussing on the way what action they should take.

'We'll just go to Smith and Elder and tell them who we are,' said Charlotte. 'And then we'll go to Mr Newby and prove to him that what he wrote was a lie. It isn't fair, Anne. He does this sort of thing all the time.'

'I wish Emily would have come too,' said Anne wistfully.

Charlotte sighed, as the train whirled them on. 'I'm afraid she's getting more and more wrapped up in herself. I can't see her ever agreeing to come to London, or anywhere else away from home. Don't you think she's getting a bit peculiar, Anne?'

'Well — she's always been different, we know that,' said Anne reluctantly, and Charlotte nodded. There was no more they could say without appearing disloyal to their sister.

★ ★ ★

Charlotte and Anne arrived, breathless and excited, at the Chapter Coffee-House in Paternoster Row, which was the only hotel in London that they knew, at eight o'clock the following morning. It was Anne's first visit to London, and she stared about her with wide eyes. They stayed for breakfast and to refresh themselves, then made their way to the offices of Smith, Elder & Co, where they asked to see Mr Smith. He was very busy that morning, and when eventually they were shown into his office and he looked up to see two little, oddly-dressed ladies, one of them wearing spectacles and holding out a letter in her hand, his irritation was hardly concealed.

He took the letter — it was his own, addressed to Currer Bell.

'Where did you get this?' he demanded

sharply, seeing that it had been opened.

'From the post-office,' said Charlotte, delighted laughter bubbling in her throat as she saw the young man's perplexity. 'It was addressed to me. We have both come so that you can see that there are at least two of us. We are three sisters — I am Charlotte Brontë, this is my sister Anne, and Ellis is my sister Emily.'

Mr Smith was too bewildered to take in what she was saying at first, then the storm broke. Mr Williams, who had corresponded so spiritedly with 'Currer Bell', was called in and introduced, and the room seemed to be full of people, all talking. The famous Currer Bell in person! It was unbelievable! And Acton too!

Charlotte became so excited by the proceedings and the reception they received that she developed a very bad nervous headache and feeling of nausea, but she was not to be allowed to rest in peace at their lodgings. After they had paid Mr Newby a visit where they told him what they thought of him, and returned to Paternoster Row, they found that Mr Smith was determined to fête his celebrated author. He arrived that evening and spirited them off to the Opera — a glittering experience for the two country girls. The following morning — being

Sunday — they were escorted to church by Mr Williams, and dined at Mr Smith's with his family, but were too exhausted and exhilarated to eat much. On the Monday, they were shown the sights, dined again with Mr Smith and had tea with Mr Williams; and on Tuesday, 11th July, they left London for the peace of home, their arms full of books, some of which were presents from Mr Smith. With what relief they sank into the seats of the railway carriage, overwhelmed by their debut into society!

★ ★ ★

Emily had been waiting patiently at the Parsonage. She had no wish to leave it, and she did not want to go out and see the world, for, as she often said, 'what would be the point? Charlotte will bring it back to me.' For Charlotte always told her of her adventures whenever she went away.

So, when they arrived at Haworth, Charlotte began an account of their doings and Emily listened eagerly, until they reached the part where she had admitted, 'We are three sisters', and Emily's brow contracted with sudden fury.

'You told them who we are? Who I am? And our names?'

'I'm sorry, Emily, it just slipped out,' said Charlotte contritely.

Emily was trembling. 'I told you I never wanted my identity revealed. No one shall ever know me as anything other than Ellis Bell. I warned you, Charlotte. How could you! There was no need to give *my* name away.'

'It was in the heat of the moment, Emily. Everything was so strange,' Anne interposed quickly.

'I'll never forgive you. I told you — I told you. I will *not* have my name bandied about. I want to be left alone.' Emily looked stormily into Charlotte's face as though she hated her, and Charlotte winced. Ever since she had read Emily's manuscripts without her permission, something had gone, some trust that had once existed between them. They were like two strangers now.

Anne bit her lip as Emily repeated fiercely, 'I'll never forgive you, Charlotte!' and ran from the room to seek the solitude that the world seemed determined to deny her, that precious solitude that was her very life.

10

On a December day in that bitter cold winter before any of the girls' novels had been accepted for publication, Charlotte opened the Parsonage door to find a sheriff's officer from Halifax standing on the doorstep.

'Yes?' she said blankly.

'I've come, Ma'am, on account of one Branwell Brontë.'

'What about Branwell?' Anxiety was written all over Charlotte's face.

'I'm afraid he must either pay immediately the debt he owes to Mr Thomas Nicholson, landlord of the Old Cock, Halifax, or come along with me.'

'Where to?' gasped Charlotte.

'York prison, Ma'am.'

Charlotte leaned heavily against the doorpost, her eyes shut. Drink was one thing — debt was another. It was inconceivable that Branwell should be taken off to prison like a common criminal!

'If you could — step into the kitchen for a moment and wait,' she managed to say, at last, 'how much does he owe?'

The man told her, and Charlotte went in

search of Emily and Anne.

'A debt-collector? Here in the house?' Anne's voice was a shocked whisper.

'We'll have to pay up for him, it's obvious,' said Emily calmly. 'Have we enough between us, Charlotte?'

'I think so, but it's so — utterly degrading,' answered Charlotte.

'Never mind. Give the man his money and let him go.' Emily, as usual, was her laconic, practical self, 'we can't do anything else.'

So that was what they did, and the incident did little to redeem Branwell in their eyes. They had watched his steady downfall from the time of Mr Robinson's death, when Mrs Robinson had stated she could have nothing further to do with him for fear of losing her inheritance. But he believed that she still loved him as passionately as he loved her, a delusion that was perpetuated by the fact that she continued to send him gifts of money — probably to keep him quiet — which he spent on drink and drugs, at the same time running up other bills he couldn't possibly pay.

He had become a pitiful figure, but Charlotte, for one, could find no more pity in her for the whining, miserable creature that had once been her brilliant brother.

'To Papa he allows rest neither day nor

night,' she wrote to Ellen, 'and he is continually screwing money out of him, sometimes threatening that he will kill himself if it is withheld from him . . . Branwell declares that he neither can nor will do anything for himself, good situations have been offered him more than once, for which, by a fortnight's work, he might have qualified himself, but he will do nothing, except drink and make us all wretched.'

Branwell had, however, still not entirely given up hope. He treasured, even now, the thought that he might make his mark in literature, and was making feeble efforts to write a long epic in verse called *Morley Hall*, but in eight months, he had not got beyond the first few pages. Charlotte swore that he was never aware that his sisters had published a line, but he could not help but notice the parcels and letters that came and went from the Parsonage, and the fact that the girls were keeping their doings a secret from him made him all the more bitter and hopeless.

Where had the good old days gone to, the days when Emily had fallen from the cherry tree as they played 'Prince Charles'; the days of Glasstown and Angria? What had happened to Charlotte, the dear friend of his childhood, with whom he had collaborated for so long on the Angrian chronicles? Charlotte looked at him now as though he did not exist, or as though he was something too contemptible for her to recognize, if she saw him in the house. Perhaps her heart would have softened towards him a little if she had been able to read his letters to his friend Leyland, the sculptor. Still mourning for his lost love, Lydia Robinson, Branwell wrote:

'*I only know that it is time for me to be something when I am nothing. That my father cannot have long to live, and that when he dies, my evening, which is already twilight, will become night — That I shall then have a constitution still so strong that it will keep me years in torture and despair when I should every hour pray that I might die — .*'

His morbid streak was growing stronger as time went on, and his behaviour grew worse. While the girls were involved in the publication of *Jane Eyre*, *Wuthering Heights* and *Agnes Grey*, Branwell lived a life of continual drinking (when he could get the money), staggering home to turn the peace of the Parsonage upside down, and then quietening himself with drops of

216

laudanum, which induced terrible dreams and nightmares that had him sweating in terror when he awoke. He had been subject to bouts of epilepsy all his life — this was the reason why Patrick had never sent him to school — and he now fell down in fits more often than ever when he was drunk.

Outside the Parsonage, he could pull himself together well enough to behave with circumspection among his friends and acquaintances, but within those four walls, the sight of his sisters and their closed circle he could no longer penetrate hurt and angered him. He was an outsider now — an unwanted burden to them — and in his misery he behaved like a child. If they could not like him, he would make sure that they hated him. That way, he would at least gain their attention. If they would not include him in their peaceful doings, he would make sure that they had no peace to carry out their schemes, whatever they were.

And what made things worse was the fact that they now had Aunt's legacy, so they were women of means, while he had been ignored, passed over, and he had nothing, only what he could beg or borrow, with no hope of being able to pay it back again!

He may have flattered himself that he had a strong constitution, but drink, drugs, and the way in which he was conducting his life were already taking a heavy toll on him, and his body was wasted, shaken, racked. His mind was almost gone, and he lived in a world of bizarre self-delusion where reality was mixed up with Angria. As it never occurred to anyone to seek medical assistance for him, he was never to recover.

Anne, to some extent, felt responsible for Branwell, and this added to the burden of guilt she already felt she carried in her sensitive soul. After all, she had been the one who had introduced him into the Robinson household at Thorp Green, and she should (she told herself) have known better, have realized that he was not armed against the ways of the world and against temptation. But how could she have foreseen what would happen?

She purged her conscience by writing, in *The Tenant of Wildfell Hall*, a stern warning to others, an unexpurgated picture of what evils could befall an unarmed man in temptation and drink. But towards Branwell himself, she felt sorrow mingled with a sort of exasperation. What had happened had not been his fault, but surely he could make *some* effort to pull himself together and endure? She, after all, had suffered a lost love too, and had led an existence that was miserable to her for many years, and she had managed to endure. Why could Branwell not do the same?

Anne was always considered by most people to be gentle, pious, and colourless, but she was no longer the innocent young girl who had set out into the world so many years ago. She had developed into a woman of character, a woman who had, as she put it, passed through 'some very unpleasant and undreamed of experiences'. Probably she was more wordly-wise than Charlotte — certainly she had suffered as much, but all beneath a veil of silence.

* * *

So what with Charlotte's cynicism and Anne's sorrowful exasperation, Emily was the only one of the three sisters who could feel some affinity with Branwell. She had told Charlotte he was a 'hopeless being'. Well, was that not what all her philosophy was about? Was not Heathcliff a hopeless being? Was not Hindley? Emily had changed her ideas a great deal since she had said, 'I despise weakness'. In herself, yes, but in others, no. She understood weakness, and from the depths of her generosity and compassion, pity came surging over her for the wreck that her brother had become. He too had had seeds of greatness in him, but life had treated him shabbily. He had achieved nothing but a most monumental failure, and failure because of flaws in character, Emily could accept and understand, as she had understood the failure of Heathcliff for precisely the same reasons.

When they were thrown together as she was writing *Wuthering Heights*, it was Branwell who had, in the model of chaos he then was, echoed down the wild and heathery corridors of the book in unmistakable accents. People had said men never spoke like Heathcliff, never behaved like Hindley, but Emily knew they were wrong, for had she not herself heard Heathcliff's voice in Branwell's violent oaths and lamentations over his lost love? Had she not seen him perform some of the actions she attributed to Hindley? He personified for her the power of love and its destructiveness, its violence and the stranglehold it could leave on the abandoned one. Such a display of emotion could not but creep into the very pores of the novel she was writing, and generate an atmosphere of frenzy and passion that was truly authentic.

So Emily helped him as much as she could. While the other girls kept away from him, Emily was his strength, the lifeline to which he clung. Not that even she could penetrate to the depths, for it was now, during the drunken nights and drug-blurred days, that the spectre of death came to haunt Branwell. On one hand, he felt he could not live, his life was so wretched — on the other, he had a deep and terrible fear of dying. The faces of Maria and Elizabeth swam before him, even in the room where his father prayed and he blasphemed, for how could the old man help him when it came to facing the Infinite alone?

Maria with her dead, cold face in her coffin — being lowered into the black earth, the dark deep pit of death — Elizabeth in the grave, the worms eating her body . . .

Panic seized him at the very thought, and he would reach unsteadily for the bottle which would help him forget, or dress himself, and stagger out to the Black Bull where there were companions, friends, lights and noise, but always, wherever he went now, the spectre of death sat on his shoulder.

Emily would wait up for him, let him into the house, and carry him upstairs when he came home drunk; she would run out the back way, through the churchyard, to knock on the window of the Bull and warn Branwell if his father was coming to fetch him home by force, but he could not tell even Emily of his fears, though he sensed her sympathy. She grieved for him with all her generous heart. She had always been the supporter of the frail, the outcast, the unwanted, and in one of her earlier poems, she had written:

'Well, some may hate, and some may scorn,
   And some may quite forget thy name,
But my sad heart must ever mourn
   Thy ruined hopes, thy blighted fame.'

'Twas thus I thought, an hour ago,
   Even weeping o'er that wretch's woe;
One word turned back my gushing tears,
   And lit my altered eye with sneers.

'Then bless the friendly dust,' I said,
'That hides thy unlamented head.
Vain as thou wert, and weak as vain,
The slave of falsehood, pride and pain,
My heart has nought akin to thine;
Thy soul is powerless over mine.'

But these were thoughts that vanished too —
   Unwise, unholy and untrue —
Do I despise the timid deer
   Because his limbs are fleet with fear?

Or would I mock the wolf's death-howl
  Because his form is gaunt and foul?
Or hear with joy the leveret's cry
  Because it cannot bravely die?

No! Then above his memory
  Let pity's heart as tender be:
Say, 'Earth lie lightly on that breast,
  And, kind Heaven, grant that spirit
rest.'*

Although she wrote it long before he
degenerated into the wreck he later became,
this poem might have been Emily's lament
for Branwell — for in spite of her sympathy,
she knew his faults. She saw quite clearly
that he was a liar, and a cheat, selfish and
self-centred. Yet she accepted him as he was,
and even felt some resentment that Charlotte
would not include him in, for instance, their
venture into poetry. It might have been just
the thing to pull him together, and there was
no doubt in Emily's mind that he had written
poems that were quite as good as some
which were included in the book of verse
they published. This was yet another grudge
that Emily bore against her sister, as well
as the intrusion on her privacy. Emily was
on Branwell's side, and she and Charlotte
seemed to have lost touch now, much to

Charlotte's hurt and bewilderment, but the more she shut Branwell out of their doings, the more Emily seemed to withdraw too.

* * *

Branwell was fast becoming seriously ill, but no medical help was sought for him. He saw no one except the local doctor, who advised him to abstain from alcohol, but laudanum had taken away his appetite, and he was so wasted that his friend John Brown (donator of the famous bag of soot for the cherry tree) laughed at him and asked whether he was wearing his father's coat. It was his own, but it hung on him like a skeleton's. He had also begun to cough badly, and, coupled with his sleeplessness, it wore him into exhaustion.

The petty measures he had to take to obtain the opiates by which he could manage to face life are expressed in this letter, scribbled hastily to his friend John Brown:

'*Dear John — I shall feel very much obliged to you if you can contrive to get me Five pence worth of Gin in a proper measure. Should it be speedily got I could perhaps take it from you or Billy at the lane top, or, what would be quite as well, sent out for, to you. I anxiously*

ask the favour because I know the good it will do me. Punctually *at Half-past Nine in the morning you will be paid the 5d out of a shilling given me then.* —
                                Yours,
                                P.B.B.'

It was now September, two months since Charlotte and Anne had paid their visit to London, and Branwell had become a terrible ruin, but no one seemed alarmed, as it had crept up on them for so long that they were used to it. Not long after the scribbled appeal to his friend John, he managed to leave his bed and stagger down to the village. William, John's brother, found him, ghastly in his gauntness and wild of eye, struggling to get home but unable to move, so the kind lad helped him to walk up the lane and into the house, an arm round his shoulders. He never left it alive again.

His death, when it came, caught all the family unprepared. They had always thought that Papa would die first, that Branwell would go on and on being a plague to them, but it was Friday, 22nd September, when he went down into the village, and he could not move from his bed for the rest of that day — nothing new to the girls. By Saturday, however, a change had come over his mind, that had been restless, agonized, full of fears and horrors.

He had previously blasphemed horribly and mocked at their humble beliefs, refused to pray with his father as the old man wrestled for his soul. Now he spoke rationally and gently, and held out his wasted hands to Patrick for comfort, admitting that he did believe, and that religion would comfort him, for he had found new faith.

He was the old Branwell back again, talking affectionately to his sisters, struggling to communicate with them. And they were only too happy, as they stood round his bed, to welcome this lost and wandering soul back into the fold. Anne had tears in her eyes, Charlotte blinked back her emotion, while Patrick rejoiced sincerely — little realizing that Branwell had never in reality been the bold, bad debaucher he had seemed. He had become so wrapped up in his Angrian world that he had constantly played a part from it, but now he stripped away the mask and revealed himself as he had always been beneath it — craving love, insecure, haunted by the fear of death and afraid for his soul. But Patrick prayed with him, and was certain he had been forgiven.

By now it was obviously only a matter of time, and on Sunday, while the family prepared for church, John Brown came to sit with his old friend. Branwell was conscious, his mind was clear.

'Oh, John,' he said, and heaved a deep sigh. 'In all my life, I've done nothing either great or good.'

Then suddenly a convulsion seized him. He grasped John's hands and gasped out, 'John — I'm dying!'

Quickly the family were called, church forgotten. The girls stood round with bowed heads in their bonnets and cloaks as Papa prayed, and heard the voice that had rung with horrible oaths whisper huskily 'Amen'. In the silence that followed, John Brown went out quietly to ring the passing bell. Branwell Brontë, aged thirty-one, had breathed his last.

★ ★ ★

His death was put down to chronic bronchitis and marasmus (wasting of the body), and it shocked the whole family. Charlotte wrote:

'I do not weep from a sense of bereavement — there is no prop withdrawn, no consolation torn away, no dear companion lost — but for the wreck of talent, the ruin of promise, the untimely dreary extinction

of what might have been a burning and shining light. My brother was a year my junior. I had aspirations and ambitions for him once, long ago — they have perished mournfully. Nothing remains of him but a memory of errors and sufferings. There is such a bitterness of pity for his life and death, such a yearning for the emptiness of his whole existence as I cannot describe.'

She herself felt the shock so badly that it made her ill. Anne grieved quietly, Emily was her usual rock-like self, prepared to administer comfort and consolation to the others, for she believed strongly in an after-life, and knew that Branwell was at peace. At least, that was how it seemed, although in her, the effect of her brother's death was to come later and in a far more terrible way than Charlotte's attack of jaundice.

So, while Charlotte lay in bed with the illness that came on immediately after Branwell's death, and Anne wept quietly, Emily seemed not to be affected. She was calm and controlled, she gave comfort and sympathy — as well as good nursing — to Charlotte so that her sister was able to recover, and she eased Anne's weeping.

Patrick too needed consolation. Charlotte recorded in a letter to Mr Williams that:

'*My poor father naturally thought more of his only son than of his daughters, and, much and long as he had suffered on his account, he cried out for his loss like David for that of Absalom — my son! my son! — and refused at first to be comforted. And then when I ought to have been able to collect my strength and be at hand to support him, I fell ill . . .*'

Yes, it was Emily who stood, steady as a rock upon her own moors, during the awful week that followed Branwell's death, and the others leaned on her, gaining strength and courage. Charlotte slowly recovered; Patrick overcame his first agonizing sense of loss and, in Charlotte's words, 'stood the storm well', while Anne regained her faith and believed that Branwell had been forgiven and was at rest, which gave her great comfort, but all was not well with Emily. Branwell's death had cut deep into her heart and mind, and its effect was seen later, after the funeral.

Branwell was buried on the Thursday, the service being conducted by Patrick's dear old friend, the Reverend William Morgan. On the next Sunday, a Funeral Service was held for the departed young man. It was the 1st October, and it was the last day of her life that Emily went out.

11

'Emily dear, shall I do it for you? You're tired.'

'Let me be.' Emily's breath rasped in her throat. 'You know I always feed the animals in the evening.'

Anne exchanged a look of helplessness with Charlotte as Emily staggered to the door and went slowly and painfully to feed the dogs.

Clouds of gloom were gathering over the Parsonage. Emily was ill — seriously ill — but she would not admit it, and there was nothing her sisters could do, for she had cut herself off from them. Their closed circle, which had seemed so impenetrable to Branwell, had had cracks appearing in it for some time. Now it was broken. Emily herself had broken it mentally, and withdrawn completely into her own mind, away from the concern and anxiety of Charlotte and Anne.

She had first become ill on the day of Branwell's funeral. The cold east wind and chilling rain of that day had soaked her as she followed the casket to the church, and sat in the damp and dreary pew throughout the service. She arrived home wet through

231

and shivering, and that night, began to cough.

All through the wet and windy month of October, her cold and cough lingered on, growing worse, and by the beginning of November, Charlotte was deeply anxious about her. Emily lost her appetite and grew thin, she coughed continually at night, trying to smother it in order not to keep the others awake, though she slept little herself, and during the day, she insisted on carrying out her chores, although it was becoming obvious that they were too much for her. But her will-power was stronger than her body. She forced herself to do the baking as usual, to feed the animals, to sit upright by the smoky fire in the evenings, though she did not write now, just sat with her work-basket, the needle seeming too heavy for her hand.

She had always been something of a mystery to the others, now she became a complete stranger, and they could do nothing but watch in terrible anxiety as she dragged herself about the house, gasping if she moved too fast, and with a hand going to her chest continually as though she had a pain there that was almost unbearable.

On November 2nd, Charlotte wrote to Mr Williams:

'*I would fain hope that Emily is a little better this evening, but it is difficult to ascertain this. She is a real stoic in illness: she neither seeks nor will accept sympathy. To put any questions, to offer any aid, is to annoy; she will not yield a step before pain or sickness till forced; not one of her ordinary avocations will she voluntarily renounce. You must look on and see her do what she is unfit to do, and not dare to say a word — a painful necessity for those to whom her health and existence are as precious as the life in their veins. When she is ill there seems to be no sunshine in the world for me. The tie of sister is near and dear indeed, and I think a certain harshness in her powerful and peculiar character only makes me cling to her more . . . *'

What did Emily think when she sat, gazing into the fire while they sat in the dining-room in the evenings? Why did she refuse help in what she must have known was her last illness? The servants of the family were convinced that she was dying of grief for her brother, but it was more complicated than that. Branwell's death, and her deep association with him beforehand had upset her dream-world. It had forced her out into reality, and now the foundations on which she had built her life were shaken. Physical illness alone might not have pulled her down so quickly as it did if her mental world had not been undermined too. For in all her life, she had never been ill (except for the odd cold or 'flu bout in the winter) unless she had been parted from home and the moors and Gondal.

But she was at home now, she had the moors within easy reach, and Gondal was hers if she chose to step into it. All this was no longer enough. Branwell had forced her out into reality, and the publication of her book had pushed her out into the world — and then rejected her. The rejection of *Wuthering Heights* had gone very deep. The world had misunderstood her, it had dismissed her ideas as rubbish, it had tried to pull her spirit down, to make her novel conform to what it felt a novel ought to be like, and Emily felt trapped, as though her soul and spirit were a hawk who had previously soared unshackled on the heights, but who had now been caught and put into a cage. It was always lack of freedom that she could not bear, and the world had imposed restrictions on her and her work, so that she could no longer write. Her identity had been revealed, and for that she would never forgive Charlotte. The happy idyll of wandering in Gondal and communing with her own personal visitations had been spoiled for her. What was left?

She clung first of all to the one thing she knew would never fail her — herself. Branwell's death and the reasons for it, to which she could find no answer; Charlotte and Anne's yearning after worldly fame and love, which she despised — all these were muddled in her head. She would turn to herself, and to nature, which had been her prop and consolation for so long. Nature would heal her — she would not let herself die — and yet — and yet — . Something in her seemed to be reaching out beyond the veil, to where all her conflicts would be stilled, all her doubts set at rest.

To die — to be at one with the Infinite which she had glimpsed so often in her visions, but which had always left her as her body pulled her back to earth — what bliss that would be. The feeling grew in her. As her frame became more and more wasted, her spirit seemed to burn brighter than ever, frightening Charlotte and Anne. She seemed to *want* to die. They could not understand it — but then, had they ever really understood her? They gazed at each other with fearful, bewildered eyes.

Later, Charlotte was to write:

'The details of her illness are deep-branded in my memory, but to dwell on them, either in thought or narrative, is not in my power. Never in all her life had she lingered over any task that lay before her, and she did not linger now. She sank rapidly. She made haste to leave us. Yet, while physically she perished, mentally she grew stronger than we had yet known her. Day by day, when I saw with what a front she met suffering, I looked on her with an anguish of wonder and love. I had seen nothing like it; but indeed, I have never seen her parallel in anything. Stronger than a man, simpler than a child, her nature stood alone. The awful point was that while full of ruth for others, on herself she had no pity; the spirit was inexorable to the flesh; from the trembling hand, the unnerved limbs, the faded eyes, the same service was exacted as they had rendered in health. To stand by and witness this, and not dare to remonstrate, was a pain no words can render.'

Charlotte plucked up her courage one morning.

'Emily dear, the doctor has come to see you.'

236

'Send him away. I'll have no poisoning doctor near me,' was Emily's brief reply. She stopped to cough.

'But, dear, he's come all this way . . . '

'Send him back, then. I'll not see him,' said Emily roughly. By now, she hardly spoke even when spoken to, such was her withdrawal into herself.

Charlotte looked at her for a moment, then went helplessly out into the hall where the local doctor was standing, a grave expression on his face as he listened to the coughing coming from the dining-room.

'I'm sorry,' she said miserably, 'I'm afraid she won't see you.'

'A great pity,' said the doctor. 'She is very ill — but you know that, don't you? From the sound of her cough, I fear she has an inflammation of the lungs.'

'Oh!' Charlotte's face was a mask of horror. 'My two eldest sisters died of that — consumption. Is that what it is? What can be done, Doctor?'

'Very little, I'm afraid, especially as she won't cooperate,' answered the doctor.

'I'm sorry,' said Charlotte again.

'Well, it can't be helped, but I don't hold out much hope for her if she neglects herself any longer,' said the doctor, as he prepared to take his leave.

When he had gone, Charlotte sank down onto a chair in the kitchen, which was empty for the moment, and hid her face in her hands. Again, as she had done time after time during these last few weeks, she faced the hideous prospect that Emily might die. Would die. Something seemed to cry out within her at the thought of losing that mysterious, harsh personality, and for a minute, she almost gave way to tears. Could she do nothing to save this sister she loved so well? The answer came back drearily. Nothing. Then one of the servants came in, and resolutely, Charlotte pulled herself together. Back inflexible, head high, she left the room.

It did not matter that during this time, Smith, Elder & Co had bought the volume of their *Poems* from the original publisher and reissued it. All Charlotte could do when they sent her the reviews was to protest in anger and grieved amazement that Emily's poems had again been ignored or misunderstood.

'Blind is he as any bat,' she wrote contemptuously of the *Spectator's* critic, 'insensate as any stone, to the merits of Ellis. He cannot feel or will not acknowledge that the very finish and *labor limae* which Currer wants, Ellis has; he is not aware that the 'true essence of poetry' pervades his compositions. Because Ellis's poems are short and abstract, the critics think them comparatively insignificant and dull. They are mistaken.'

Emily did not even bother to glance at the reviews. She was no longer interested in what the world had to say about her.

★ ★ ★

By the end of November, Charlotte was making final, desperate efforts to save Emily at all costs. She could no longer bear to lie awake night after night listening to that deep, harsh cough; watching Emily, a wraith in her frailty and fever, trying to perform her duties during the day, but by now almost unable to move about the house. Only her phenomenal willpower enabled her to do anything, but still she insisted on behaving as normally as possible, to the terrible distress of Anne and Charlotte.

Charlotte wrote to a famous homoeopathic physician, Dr Epps, on the advice of Mr Williams, giving details of Emily's case, as her sister continued to refuse all medical help. The 'symptoms of her malady' are given as follows:

'Her appetite failed; she evinced a continual thirst, with a craving for acids, and required a constant change of beverage. In appearance she grew rapidly emaciated. Her pulse — the only time she allowed it to be felt — was found to be 115 per minute. The patient usually appeared worse in the forenoon, she was then frequently exhausted and drowsy; towards evening, she often seemed better.

'Expectoration accompanies the cough. The shortness of breath is aggravated by the slightest exertion. The patient's sleep is supposed to be tolerably good at intervals, but disturbed by paroxysms of coughing. Her resolution to contend against illness being very fixed, she has never consented to lie in bed for a single day — she sits up from 7 in the morning till 10 at night. All medical aid she has rejected, insisting that Nature should be left to take her own course. She has taken no medicine . . . Her diet, which she regulates herself, is simple and light.

'The patient has hitherto enjoyed pretty good health, although she has never looked strong, and the family constitution is not supposed to be robust. Her temperament is highly nervous. She has been accustomed to a sedentary and studious life.'

Anxiously, Charlotte sent off this letter and waited for the eminent doctor's reply, but she knew already in her heart that it was hopeless. All her letters to Ellen and Mr Williams written during this period show a deep despair and bewilderment that Emily could do this to her and to her sorrowing family. If *only* she would be more tractable — yet it was her very intractability that made Charlotte cling to her all the more closely.

'I believe if you were to see her, your impression would be that there is no hope,' she wrote despairingly to Ellen. 'Our position is, and has been for some weeks, exquisitely painful. God only knows how all this is to terminate.'

And, 'I *do* wish I knew her state of mind and feelings more clearly,' she cried piteously, but Emily was revealing nothing.

To Mr Williams, she confided, 'I can give no favourable report of Emily's state. My father is very despondent about her . . . He shakes his head and speaks of others in our family once similarly afflicted, for whom he likewise persisted in hoping against hope, and who are now removed where hope and fear fluctuate no more.'

The loss of his only son and his recollections of Maria and Elizabeth's illnesses had obviously broken Patrick's spirit so that he could not even hope regarding Emily. He could only sit in his study and pray that her passing would be as painless as possible, while Charlotte and Anne — the latter beginning to show signs of illness herself, which distressed Emily — tried to hold on to some form of hope and consolation.

Eventually, Dr Epps replied, in language that Charlotte could not understand, sending medicine, but Emily refused even to try it. She was now so frail that it was a miracle she was still alive. On the evening of Monday, 18th December, 1848, she slowly rose from her chair and went to give the dogs their supper of an apronful of broken meat and bread. Charlotte and Anne followed her, and saw her stagger and reel against the wall, but she would not let them help her. She insisted on giving the animals their food herself. Afterwards, Charlotte read to her from a book of Emerson's *Essays*.

'I read till I found she was not listening,' Charlotte told Mr Williams. 'Next day, the first glance at her face told me what would happen before nightfall.'

Emily insisted on rising as usual, and dressing herself, which she did with many a pause for breath, and to cough. She came slowly and painfully down the stairs and into the dining-room, where Anne was dusting, and Charlotte was writing to Ellen. Her eyes were glazed, and her breath caught in her throat. Yet she still took up her work and made some attempt to sew.

Silently, Charlotte looked at her, and then continued her writing.

'Moments so dark as these I have never known. I pray for God's support to us all. Hitherto He has granted it — .'

By the time the letter had been posted, it was almost noon, and Emily was growing worse. The pain was terrible. Yet she would not go to bed, only consented to lie down on the old horsehair sofa. Death was in her face, and at last, she gasped out to Charlotte, 'If you will send for a doctor, I will see him now.'

But before one could be brought, about two o'clock, Emily fell back after her struggle for breath, drained, and her soul flew up to meet and mingle with her God.

Epilogue

She had died of consumption, of two months duration. When she was taken upstairs and laid out on her narrow bed, the house seemed unnaturally quiet, except that her great dog Keeper lay outside her bedroom door and howled mournfully, as though he knew she was gone. When her coffin was carried out to the church, Keeper followed at Mr Brontë's heels, and lay silent in the aisle throughout the service. Anne and Charlotte clung together; Patrick murmured, time and time again, 'Charlotte, you must bear up — I shall sink if you fail me.'

Emily was gone.

They would never hear her cheerful whistle any more, never see her striding across the moors she had loved with Keeper at her side. It was as though a part of them had been cut away.

The day after the funeral, Charlotte sat down and wrote to Ellen, 'Emily suffers no more from pain or weakness now. She will never suffer more in this world. She is gone, after a short, hard conflict. She died on *Tuesday*, the very day I wrote to you.

I thought it very possible she might be with us for weeks; and a few hours afterwards, she was in eternity. Yes, there is no Emily in time or earth now. Yesterday we put her poor, wasted mortal frame quietly under the church pavement. We are very calm at present. Why should we be otherwise? The anguish of seeing her suffer is over; the spectacle of the pains of death is gone by; the funeral day is past. We feel she is at peace.'

And to Mr Williams, on Christmas Day, as though laying a wreath of flowers gently on her sister's resting-place, Charlotte wrote:

'Some sad comfort I take, as I hear the wind blow and feel the cutting keenness of the frost, in knowing that the elements cannot reach her grave — her fever is quieted, her restlessness soothed, her deep, hollow cough is hushed for ever; we do not hear it in the night nor listen for it in the morning; we have not the conflict of the strangely strong spirit and the fragile frame before us — relentless conflict — once seen, never to be forgotten . . .

'So I will not now ask why Emily was torn from us in the fulness of our attachment, rooted up in the prime of her own days, in the promise of her

245

powers — why her existence now lies like a field of green corn trodden down — like a tree in full bearing — struck at the root; I will only say, sweet is rest after labour and calm after tempest, and repeat again and again that Emily knows that now.'

Looking for Emily

In her lifetime, Emily Brontë was misinter-preted, misunderstood, dismissed as an inferior writer to Charlotte. But in the years that followed her death, the reading public paid penance, and elevated her to a pinnacle where she stands alone, her one great book unequalled by any other because it is in a category as well as a class, of its own.

When any icon has died, followers are certain that if they had been there at the time, misunderstandings would never have occurred, and any tragedy would never have happened. Yet would we have understood Emily any better than her contemporaries? Would we have found her more congenial, managed to make friends with her and pierce her reserve. Would we have treated her any better?

Almost a century and a half after Emily's death (in 1997, actually), the literary world celebrated the publication of such Victorian masterpieces as *Wuthering Heights, Jane Eyre and Thackeray's Vanity Fair* by holding its own 'Booker Prize' for the year 1847. *Wuthering Heights* was one of the novels on the short list, along with, amongst others, *Jane Eyre* and *Agnes Grey*. But the winner, which might well have been the popular favourite if the readers and critics of the Victorian world had been able to vote, was Thackeray, with *Vanity Fair*.

It seems that Emily Brontë is destined always to remain mysteriously in the shadows, her genius recognised and undisputed, yet never reaching that pinnacle afforded to other, less complex — or perhaps, less *simple* — writers. Since her death, few seekers of her shade have been able to pin her down, as it were, and confront the real woman herself.

With this in mind, I set out on a literary pilgrimage to try and find her. I had, as a professional novelist and non-fiction writer, written books about the family, involving immense and detailed research, it was true, but this time I decided to investigate as my own personal self, just an ordinary woman at the end of the 20th century, on the verge of the 21st. I wanted to discover Emily as she is today, what she means to the average person in the street, to the average reader and library borrower. Has Emily survived? And what about her writing? What does her work give to us today, and what is she herself to us now?

★ ★ ★

The Brontës — and Emily just as much as Charlotte, though not quite so recognisably Anne, perhaps — are certainly very much in evidence as part of our everyday life. They can be found in every place where 'classic' novels are represented, and the scant facts of their lives are far better known to the general public than the facts of the lives of such writers as Thackeray or Mrs Gaskell, their contemporaries. Their writing is set study for examinations, it is public property in the same way as the work of Dickens. But quite often, mistakes in Brontë identity occur exactly as they did when the books first came out.

'Emily Brontë? Oh, yes, didn't she write *Jane Eyre*?'

'The Brontës? Oh, I didn't know there were three of them.'

'*Wuthering Heights* — yes, it was written by Charlotte Brontë, wasn't it?'

At random, I enquired of Graham Poven, the man who came to service the gas fires, what Emily Brontë meant to him, personally. He grinned.

'She's a writer, isn't she?'

'Do you know anything about her work?' I asked. 'Her writing?' There was a long

249

pause, then I prompted:

'*Wuthering Heights?*'

'Heathcliff and all that?'

'Yes.'

'No, it doesn't mean a thing to me really.'

Even those who have enjoyed and remembered the novels cannot always recollect which novel is which. The mad woman of *Jane Eyre* somehow becomes a character of Emily's, while Thrushcross Grange and Wildfell Hall loom vaguely as common backgrounds, though lesser known than Thornfield. The sisters' three best known works may be clear, but when it comes to their 'other' novels, the public may well be quite at a loss.

So although they are recognised as authors of classic works of English literature, the girls still remain mysterious figures isolated behind their common surname (though in a different way, of course, to the days when they were completely unknown.) The names are still confusing in their similarity. Then, it was Bell — now it is Brontë, but even so, to the general public, it is much the same.

And although Emily has had her champions, yet still as a person, she might as well be living today in the depth of the Yorkshire moors, a reclusive figure who never — in the modern parlance — takes part in PR exercises or makes public appearances. If she lived today, we can be sure we would never see her on breakfast TV talking about her 'latest novel', though her sister Charlotte would certainly have enjoyed crossing swords with the lions of the literary world on arts programmes, and perhaps attending literary dinners, as an honoured celebrity guest.

★ ★ ★

Right from the early days, there were pilgrims who were interested enough to trek into the wilds of 'Brontë Country' (even without the benefit of conducted coach tours), poking an inquisitive nose into the Black Bull at Haworth, eying the uncompromising Parsonage building, crowding into the Church. Now, travellers come from all over the world to the tiny moorland village, making it one of the great literary shrines. We can examine the lives of the girls under a microscope, as it were, their secrets laid bare, even Charlotte's wedding bonnet and the sofa on which Emily breathed her last.

But where is Emily, in all this hype? I found her on the library shelves, yes, in copies of *Wuthering Heights* in all sections

251

marked 'Classics' in bookshops. And yet, she is still elusive. *Wuthering Heights* can be grasped, but not its author. No-one really knows any more about Emily than they did when her work first appeared. There has been conjecture, millions of words of appreciation, interpretation, examination, yet Emily herself is still tantalisingly out of reach.

* * *

Not that the public in general has not tried very hard to capture her. At this time, approaching the end of the century following her death, there are well over a hundred books listed for the reference of the general enquirer as 'in print' on the subject of the Brontë family, Brontë sisters and their literary achievements. The subjects range from 'straight' biography to assessments of the genius of Emily and Beethoven, for example, or Emily and Thomas Hardy.

But this is only the tip, as it were, of the iceberg. Specialised works have been written on all possible aspects of the Brontës and their work, and the interest in them shows no sign of abating. People will still be writing books on the Brontës as the end of the world dawns, even though the usual cry of publishers is that there are 'far too

252

many on the Brontës as it is'. And readers will still be reading them, the mystery will never be solved, the end of the story will never be reached.

It might well be said that Emily, the person, can be found in the many books that have been written about her. They range from *A Life of Emily Brontë* by Edward Chitham (Basil Blackwell, 1987) to *Emily Brontë: A Psychological Portrait* by Norma Crandall (R. R. Smith, 1957), *Emily Brontë: the Artist as a Free Woman* by Stevie Davies (Carcanet Press Ltd, 1983), *Emily Brontë; A Chainless Soul* by Katherine Frank (Hamish Hamilton, 1990), *Emily Brontë: A Biography* by Winifred Gerin (Clarendon Press, 1971), etc, etc. Literally hundreds of books have been written exploring the life, the mind, the character, the work, of this one shy, reclusive woman. I myself have written *The Brontë Sisters' Search for Love*, which contains a detailed study of Emily as well as Charlotte and Anne, and involved years of research and thought, in addition to this novel about Emily's life.

But it seems that out of all the sisters, Emily is the most inscrutable, the most difficult to get to know, even though the facts of her life were basically extremely simple. There were no mysterious excursions, or unexplained visits, or letters from people who have not been identified. There was not even, for Emily, the interweaving with others, strangers, foreigners, such as happened when Charlotte attempted to carry on her correspondence with M. Heger, and the letters passed into the keeping of his wife. Emily stands still, as she stood in her lifetime, alone against the familiar background of home and family. The clues are known, they are there for anyone to read. And yet, nobody even today really feels they have reached a satisfactory understanding of her.

The books which have been written have studied over and over again, various aspects of her personality, and she has been dissected so much that one might think nothing can possibly remain to be said. Yet it is Emily, not Anne or Charlotte, who remains still the most enigmatic of enigmas. No-one, even those who have written about her, really feel they know her well.

★ ★ ★

We can make a start, though, with the books which have tried to pin her down on paper and to catch the elusive butterfly quality of her writing in a net, as it were, pinning it, glorious wings outspread, for all to see, even if they can actually give us only the most cursory introduction to Emily Brontë today. Many of them are the result of far more than the normal amount of research and dedication to the subject of a biography or an appreciation. The author Winifred Gerin, for instance, lived for years actually in Haworth itself, soaking in, as it were, the atmosphere and breathing the very air the Brontës had breathed. She produced biographies of all three of the famous sisters and her book *Charlotte Brontë: The Evolution of Genius* was awarded several literary awards and prizes.

Emily herself — as well as the other girls — has been portrayed on stage and film, as well as radio, more times than one might imagine, but there does not seem to be any well-known definitive portrayal of her. By 'definitive', I mean something that has passed into public awareness as the 1939 film of *Wuthering Heights*, starring Laurence Olivier as the broodingly Byronic Heathcliff, for instance, passed. But there have been dramatic attempts to recreate not only the novels of the Brontës, but the life of the family itself, for the public's interested gaze, almost since the books were written.

The first work to appear on the stage in dramatised form was Charlotte's *Jane Eyre,* which was mounted in both London and New York (where, we must not forget, the 'Bell' novels had caused the equivalent of best-selling tabloid sensationalism) at the end of the 1840s. There were at least six further stage productions during the 19th century, and more than thirty more up to the present time. All the books were dramatised, and there have been radio, TV and film versions.

Jane Eyre and *Wuthering Heights* lead the field, however. Information available from The Brontë Society, which has its headquarters at the Parsonage, Haworth, the Brontë home, informs us of just a few of the dramatic adaptations of *Wuthering Heights*, and the list is an impressive one. The earliest film version, made in 1920 and filmed (unlike most of the others) actually on location around Haworth, seems to have sunk without trace so far as public memory is concerned. Big names in the cast included Milton Rosmer as Heathcliff, Annie Trevor as Catherine, Louis B Furniss as Edgar Linton and Alice de Winton as Mrs Linton. An interesting actress who appeared as young Catherine was called Twinks Kenyon.

In 1939 the United Artists/Metro Goldwyn Mayer film of *Wuthering Heights*, directed by William Wyler and starring Laurence

Olivier and Merle Oberon as Heathcliff and Catherine, appeared in a storm of Hollywood hype and was hailed as a brilliant masterpiece. When I had the opportunity to see this film, some forty years after its release, I was expecting an experience I would never forget, but I have to admit that I was strangely disappointed. The ballroom scenes, with their huge crinolines, and lovely women, were wonderful — but there are no ballroom scenes in the *Wuthering Heights* that I read. And though Laurence Olivier made a staggering, sensual, earthy impact as Heathcliff, he was not Heathcliff as I visualised him. Neither was Merle Oberon anything like my image of Catherine.

This can partly be explained because of the Hollywood setting (the film was shot entirely on the set with fake, imported heather 'moors') and the fact that Miss Oberon, by all accounts, was wonderfully beautiful but no great actress. Also by the show-biz gossip about things that became legend during the shooting of the film. Laurence Olivier had apparently wanted Vivien Leigh to play Catherine (Miss Leigh too wanted the role) and as a result of having to play opposite Miss Oberon instead, he found his irritation and annoyance at working with her increased until they were barely on speaking terms. The touching death scene where Heathcliff and Catherine gasp out their undying love with tears streaming down their faces, in each other's arms, must have been ironical to watch, since the two players were anything but *sympatico* to each other, and the 'tears' were in fact huge dollops of green glycerine, which was used on film sets at that time for faking deeply emotional weeping. I had to admit, though, that if Emily Brontë had been aware of this sort of thing taking place during the filming of her book, she would probably have appreciated it very much, since she had a robust sense of irony and humour. Not for Emily the romantic rose-tinted spectacle vision of her hero and heroine. She knew them for what they were, fallible human beings, and would have felt quite at home, I think, with the backbiting enmities and loves of Tinseltown.

Other versions of *Wuthering Heights* have appeared on TV, and these include one in 1948 that starred Keiron Moore and Katharine Blake as Heathcliff and Catherine, and one in 1953 with Richard Todd and Yvonne Mitchell as the lovers. In 1962, yet another TV version appeared, with Keith Michell and Claire Bloom in the lead roles, and in 1967, Ian McShane and Angela Scoular brought their interpretive powers into play. In 1978 there was yet another TV version, this time a serial, starring Ken Hutchinson and Kay Adshead.

In the meantime, the film-makers had not been idle. Everyone has their own idea about the 'real', the authentic, the true Heathcliff, the true Catherine — which is probably why I was not really satisfied with Laurence Olivier's admittedly masterly Heathcliff in the 1939 film version. Just like their creator, Heathcliff and Catherine are insubstantial, and any attempt to pin them down is doomed, overall, to fail. But there were some gallant attempts made in 1970 and 1992, when two feature films appeared with the same irresistible title — *Wuthering Heights*. The 1970 cast included Timothy Dalton and Anna Calder-Marshall, with Judy Cornwell as Nelly, and in 1992 the main parts were taken by Ralph Fiennes and Juliette Binoche, with Janet McTeer as Nelly Dean.

Other versions of Emily's novel have been made (to mention just a few) in Mexico and Bombay, and there has even been a ballet mounted by Ballet National de Marseille in 1982, with the fascinating title *Les Hauts de Hurlevent: histoire d'une passion* (Wuthering Heights of course, but how intriguingly translated, including the untranslatable Yorkshire word 'wuthering', into French). Nevertheless, in spite of the dedication and effort and the star names who have appeared in a long procession over the years as the ill-fated Heathcliff and the doomed Catherine, there is, as I have said, no really successful interpretation of Emily's book, one which really does it justice and lives as, for instance, the sweeping film of *Gone with the Wind* has recognisably lived, for several generations, showing no sign that it will become any less or any dated than it was when it first triumphantly took the world by storm.

Part of the reason why it is difficult to capture Emily's writing has to be because though the novel does not fail to move the reader powerfully when read aloud — even in serial form — this is due to the fact that Emily is speaking to us in her own words. Try to impose some other dramatic framework on the book, though, and the structure of the novel itself becomes cumbersome and awkward, a challenge for any dramatist.

TV and film fare a little better because the cameras can go out of doors and move about, as free as the characters in the novel, over heath and rock, skimming the surface of the earth as this book does, but there are remarkably few stage versions of *Wuthering Heights* ever to have even been attempted, and almost none successfully. Every dramatist who is challenged by *Wuthering Heights* and wants to make it into a play has had to face up to the fact that, essentially, it cannot be portrayed on a stage. Emily captures air and space, movement of the wind of the heath, clouds, storms and lightning — in an essence, freedom from the earth into shadows and the spirit — within the pages of her book. And no playwright can successfully achieve this in a theatre.

The story is told in such a way that if Emily had tried to make it difficult to capture on purpose, she could not have done better. For the action of the plot contains several highly important scenes which, dramatically, must be shown as they happen, even though this is impossible, in order for the story to work at all. One of these, the most famous 'set piece' scene, is the midnight escapade on the heath, where Catherine and Heathcliff spy on the family at Thrushcross Grange through a window, and are attacked by dogs. Heathcliff escapes, but Catherine has to be left behind, injured.

Unless a complete mock-up of the moors, the two houses, the Grange and the Heights, are brought onto the stage, complete with dogs and night and all the other required effects, it is very difficult to find a workable way in which this part of the story can be told at all. A clever dramatist, of course, will find a way round such stumbling-blocks, and I have seen dramatisations which — for instance — left the scene out and had the whole episode recounted by Heathcliff when he returned to the Heights. But the tale told at second hand, even by a glowering, smouldering actor who, so far as looks went, made quite a creditable Heathcliff, was completely lifeless, even boring. All the vital life was missing, because we had not witnessed the scene for ourselves.

The few word-portraits of Emily, including those for the stage, for her portrayal by an actress — the best known stage version being, possibly, the play *Wild Decembers* by Clemence Dane — leave us with the feeling that they too are somehow unreal and unearthly. Emily was such a peculiar person that even to try and give her the attributes of an 'ordinary' woman strikes an immediate wrong note. But yet, how does a writer or dramatist begin from the premise that the character they want to recreate was 'peculiar'? Emily was not peculiar to herself, and quite certainly would have regarded everyone else, rather than herself, as odd.

I can remember, as a teenager attending Speech and Drama Classes, once being given the part of Emily Brontë in some scene which dealt with Emily's death, and the dramatic moments previous to it. The dialogue was, as far as the playwright could keep it, in Emily's own words and the recollections of Charlotte. I have to admit that (particularly in view of my age then) I found the character of Emily almost impossible to visualise. When we alternated parts, I was much more at home with the far easier character of Charlotte — or even Anne. Emily seemed to speak and exist in melodramatic cliches.

I interviewed actress Paula Anthony, who has had wide experience of portraying people on the professional stage. She revealed that: 'I have never taken part in anything about, or by the Brontës. There are not many opportunities — though I have known of several productions, notably one in recent years at Theatr Clwyd in North Wales, of *Jane Eyre*. It was very visual and atmospheric, but I know several regular theatregoers who said they didn't find it altogether successful.'

I asked Paula how she thought she would tackle the task of portraying Emily on the stage.

'Well, I would want to do my own research into any character I had to play, but obviously, with the demands of a busy schedule, repertory and so on, and also considering what information was in the script, there would be only a limited amount of time available, I would not be able to dig as deeply as a novelist might, or a research worker. I have done some research, just to give you some idea, and I found that on the surface, to the outside world, there is very little to go on with regard to Emily's character. In such a case, it is very important to approach the part from within, more than I might have to do with someone who gave a lot away.'

My next question: 'Would you like to play Emily?'

'I'd look on it — because she hasn't been represented very often — as a great privilege as well as a challenge. I would feel I'd want to do a certain amount of pioneering work. I would like to give her some new dimension and offer a new or unusual side of her character.'

'Do you think there were other sides — more to her than the Emily we mostly visualise?'

'Yes, I do. But at the same time I'd like to think that the script would give an actress a margin to exercise a certain amount of freedom in her portrayal.'

'Would it bother you that Emily seems to

have been a mystic? Would that make it more difficult?'

'No, not for me. It is just one aspect of herself.'

'What about convincing an audience?'

'I think Emily had her feet so much on the ground as well that an audience would take the whole person without trouble.'

Paula pointed out that an actress approaches a period role partly through the costume that person would have worn — particularly, as many other actors and actresses have agreed, through the footwear. In Emily's case, the voluminous skirts and boots would have provided their own restrictions to an essentially free spirit.

'I am sure she felt this, and it would be a mistake to try to lift her from her historical setting,' she added.

★ ★ ★

This is a very relevant comment, for though Emily has a universal, even a cosmic appeal, she was confined within the body and lifetime of a Victorian woman, for better or for worse, and we cannot actually bring her into our own time and re-locate her in the Britain of today. Essentially, she has to remain not only an enigma, but an anachronism.

265

The truth was that Emily was not only *not* good material for a writer or playwright, but she lacked the element of sympathy or empathy, which would have made readers or audiences warm to her. Emily was, generally, not very likeable in the popularly accepted emotional sense. She was too prickly, too awkward, too difficult to fathom out let alone understand. And even if the reader succeeded in getting close enough to her to know what she was thinking and feeling, the awareness would in all probability have made him uneasy, rather than endeared him to her. Emily's thoughts were, to the average person, far too tough and uncompromising, with no softness or desire to please about them. Consequently, any attempt to portray her as truthfully as possible will in all likelihood inevitably meet with disinterest, or even dislike, in the average person.

* * *

So what are we left with? Emily's actual physical remains, the place where her body lies at rest. Only Anne, of all of them, was buried away from Haworth, and Emily sleeps beneath the floor of her father's church in the village — that church which, together with the teeming, cholera-inducing graveyard, was

266

always visible like a silent warning, outside the Parsonage windows. The church was rebuilt after the time of the Brontës, and it is not possible to view Emily's actual grave, but the memorial plaque in the church, to the whole family, reads as follows:

In memory of
Maria, wife of the Revd P. Brontë A.B. Minister of Haworth
She died Septr 15th 1821, in the 39th year of her age.
Also of Maria their daughter: who died May 6th 1825. In the 12th year of her age.
Also of Elizabeth, their daughter; who died June 15th 1825, in the 11th year of her age.
Also of Patrick Branwell their son: who died Septr 24th 1848, aged 31 years.
Also of Emily Jane, their daughter: who died Decr 19th 1848, aged 30 years.
Also of Anne, their daughter: who died May 28th 1849, aged 30 years:
she was buried at the Old Church Scarborough.
Also of Charlotte. their daughter. Wife of the Revd A. B. Nicholls, B.A.
She died March 31st 1855, in the 39th year of her age.
Also of the aforenamed Revd P. Brontë

A.B. who died June 7th 1861. In the 85th year of his age; having been Incumbent of Haworth for upwards of 41 years.

'The sting of death is sin, and the strength of sin is the law. but thanks be to God, which giveth us the victory through our Lord Jesus Christ. 1 Cor. XV. 56.57.'

So, surrounded by the family which clung so close in life, we might imagine that Emily, traditionally, will be found here. Except, of course, that anyone who has ever stood in the lane that runs beside the Parsonage, from the village and the church to the open moors beyond, as I did, will be aware that this is not so. Emily had fled, as soon as her spirit was free, up this lane which she had passed so many times in her life, seeking the wide space and sky, the colours of the heath and all the teeming existence that was there for her then. And that is where we who perhaps want to pursue her beyond the prickly, awkward, secretive yet incredibly open and honest image she used to shield herself and her genius as a writer while she lived, will find her now.

Grateful thanks to Katherine White, Assistant Curator and Librarian, Brontë Parsonage Museum, Haworth, for her assistance and for information.

Dilys Gater

Books by Dilys Gater
Published by The House of Ulverscroft:

PREJUDICED WITNESS
THE DEVIL'S OWN
SOPHY
A BOOK CASE: A POPULAR AUTHOR'S
SUCCESS STORY
THE DARK STAR
THE LURE OF THE FALCON
THE EMILY EXPERIMENT
PROPHECY FOR A QUEEN
A PLACE OF SAFETY
THE WITCH-GIRL
THE BRONTË SISTERS' SEARCH FOR LOVE

Under the Name of Dilys Gater
& Terry Roche:

THE YEAR'S AT THE SPRING

Under the Name of Dilys Gater
& Richard Lawler:

ZODIAC

THE GREENWAY
Jane Adams

When Cassie and her twelve-year-old cousin Suzie had taken a short cut through an ancient Norfolk pathway, Suzie had simply vanished . . . Twenty years on, Cassie is still tormented by nightmares. She returns to Norfolk, determined to solve the mystery.

FORTY YEARS
ON THE WILD FRONTIER
Carl Breihan & W. Montgomery

Noted Western historian Carl Breihan has culled from the handwritten diaries of John Montgomery, grandfather of co-author Wayne Montgomery, new facts about Wyatt Earp, Doc Holliday, Bat Masterson and other famous and infamous men and women who gained notoriety when the Western Frontier was opened up.

TAKE NOW, PAY LATER
Joanna Dessau

This fiction based on fact is the love-turning-to-hate story of Robert Carr, Earl of Somerset, and his wife, Frances.

McLEAN AT THE GOLDEN OWL
George Goodchild
Inspector McLean has resigned from Scotland Yard's CID and has opened an office in Wimpole Street. With the help of his able assistant, Tiny, he solves many crimes, including those of kidnapping, murder and poisoning.

KATE WEATHERBY
Anne Goring
Derbyshire, 1849: The Hunter family are the arrogant, powerful masters of Clough Grange. Their feuds are sparked by a generation of guilt, despair and ill-fortune. But their passions are awakened by the arrival of nineteen-year-old Kate Weatherby.

A VENETIAN RECKONING
Donna Leon
When the body of a prominent international lawyer is found in the carriage of an intercity train, Commissario Guido Brunetti begins to dig deeper into the secret lives of the once great and good.

A TASTE FOR DEATH
Peter O'Donnell

Modesty Blaise and Willie Garvin take on impossible odds in the shape of Simon Delicata, the man with a taste for death, and Swordmaster, Wenczel, in a terrifying duel. Finally, in the Sahara desert, the intrepid pair must summon every killing skill to survive.

SEVEN DAYS FROM MIDNIGHT
Rona Randall

In the Comet Theatre, London, seven people have good reason for wanting beautiful Maxine Culver out of the way. Each one has reason to fear her blackmail. But whose shadow is it that lurks in the wings, waiting to silence her once and for all?

QUEEN OF THE ELEPHANTS
Mark Shand

Mark Shand knows about the ways of elephants, but he is no match for the tiny Parbati Barua, the daughter of India's greatest expert on the Asian elephant, the late Prince of Gauripur, who taught her everything. Shand sought out Parbati to take part in a film about the plight of the wild herds today in north-east India.

THE DARKENING LEAF
Caroline Stickland

On storm-tossed Chesil Bank in 1847, the young lovers, Philobeth and Frederick, prevent wreckers mutilating the apparent corpse of a young woman. Discovering she is still alive, Frederick takes her to his grandmother's home. But the rescue is to have violent and far-reaching effects . . .

A WOMAN'S TOUCH
Emma Stirling

When Fenn went to stay on her uncle's farm in Africa, the lovely Helena Starr seemed to resent her — especially when Dr Jason Kemp agreed to Fenn helping in his bush hospital. Though it seemed Jason saw Fenn as little more than a child, her feelings for him were those of a woman.

A DEAD GIVEAWAY
Various Authors

This book offers the perfect opportunity to sample the skills of five of the finest writers of crime fiction — Clare Curzon, Gillian Linscott, Peter Lovesey, Dorothy Simpson and Margaret Yorke.

DOUBLE INDEMNITY — MURDER FOR INSURANCE
Jad Adams

This is a collection of true cases of murderers who insured their victims then killed them — or attempted to. Each tense, compelling account tells a story of cold-blooded plotting and elaborate deception.

THE PEARLS OF COROMANDEL
By Keron Bhattacharya

John Sugden, an ambitious young Oxford graduate, joins the Indian Civil Service in the early 1920s and goes to uphold the British Raj. But he falls in love with a young Hindu girl and finds his loyalties tragically divided.

WHITE HARVEST
Louis Charbonneau

Kathy McNeely, a marine biologist, sets out for Alaska to carry out important research. But when she stumbles upon an illegal ivory poaching operation that is threatening the world's walrus population, she soon realises that she will have to survive more than the harsh elements . . .

TO THE GARDEN ALONE
Eve Ebbett

Widow Frances Morley's short, happy marriage was childless, and in a succession of borders she attempts to build a substitute relationship for the husband and family she does not have. Over all hovers the shadow of the man who terrorized her childhood.

CONTRASTS
Rowan Edwards

Julia had her life beautifully planned — she was building a thriving pottery business as well as sharing her home with her friend Pippa, and having fun owning a goat. But the goat's problems brought the new local vet, Sebastian Trent, into their lives.

MY OLD MAN AND THE SEA
David and Daniel Hays

Some fathers and sons go fishing together. David and Daniel Hays decided to sail a tiny boat seventeen thousand miles to the bottom of the world and back. Together, they weave a story of travel, adventure, and difficult, sometimes terrifying, sailing.

SQUEAKY CLEAN
James Pattinson

An important attribute of a prospective candidate for the United States presidency is not to have any dirt in your background which an eager muckraker can dig up. Senator William S. Gallicauder appeared to fit the bill perfectly. But then a skeleton came rattling out of an English cupboard.

NIGHT MOVES
Alan Scholefield

It was the first case that Macrae and Silver had worked on together. Malcolm Underdown had brutally stabbed to death Edward Craig and had attempted to murder Craig's fiancée, Jane Harrison. He swore he would be back for her. Now, four years later, he has simply walked from the mental hospital. Macrae and Silver must get to him — before he gets to Jane.

GREATEST CAT STORIES
Various Authors

Each story in this collection is chosen to show the cat at its best. James Herriot relates a tale about two of his cats. Stella Whitelaw has written a very funny story about a lion. Other stories provide examples of courageous, clever and lucky cats.